Pisgah Press was established in 2011 to publish and promote works of quality offering original ideas and insight into the human condition and the world around us.

Copyright © 2023 Harry N. Hirsch

Published by Pisgah Press, LLC
PO Box 9663, Asheville, NC 28815
www.pisgahpress.com

Book design: A. D. Reed, MyOwnEditor.com

Library of Congress Cataloging-in-Publication Data
Hirsch, Harry N.
.
Fault Line/H.N. Hirsch
Library of Congress Control Number: 2022950684

ISBN: 978-1-942016-76-2
First Edition
June 2023
Printed in the United States of America

Fault Line

H. N. Hirsch

Pisgah Press
Asheville, NC
IP

1

On his first day in California, Bob Abramson awoke to an earthquake, rain, and murder.

The clock radio went off just as a mellow California voice was announcing "a small earthquake." For a moment Bob didn't know where he was. His heart raced.

He quickly glanced at his Filofax, open on the bedside table. Saturday, July 8, 1989. He remembered where he was and what he was doing in this strange room with suitcases and boxes spread out all over the floor. He took a few deep breaths.

Marcus must have set the alarm, although why, Bob couldn't fathom.

Bob had flown in the night before. Marcus had scurried to come out a few days sooner to meet the movers, who arrived ahead of schedule from the East.

He pulled himself out of bed and wondered what you were supposed to do after an earthquake. Having grown up and gone to school on the East coast, he was terrified of earthquakes, not to mention mud slides and fires, all the things he knew were possible in southern California beneath the placid, gorgeous surface.

He glanced around the room, where nothing seemed to have moved, then peered out the window. A drizzle was coming down but everything was still in place, all the houses and lawns and cars neat and tidy, just as they had been when they looked at the house a few months before.

His panic subsided.

He looked at the clock radio: *6:30*. The mellow voice was explaining that the quake was "only" a 3.2, nothing to worry about, no damage reported. He trudged to the bathroom, tripping over an open suitcase.

When he came out he could smell Marcus's scrambled eggs. He pulled on gym shorts and a T-shirt as he walked into the kitchen. He kissed the back of Marcus's neck and announced, "We've had a small earthquake."

"You mean last night?" Marcus smiled. Having been separated for a few days and exhausted with packing for a week before that, they both had been more than ready for affection.

Bob smiled. "No, a real one. It was on the radio. Three-point-two. I guess that counts as little. No damage. But what is this rain? I thought this was sunny California."

Marcus chuckled as Bob added pepper to the eggs. Marcus always forgot the pepper.

"It's called June Gloom," Marcus said. "Someone explained it to me. The desert east of here heats up fast as warmer weather arrives, pulls in mist from the ocean, so for a while there can be gray skies or drizzle. Or something like that. Topography. It can start in May and doesn't end until around now."

"My first day, rain and an earthquake."

"Don't be a grouch. There's coffee. This will be done in two minutes."

Marcus had met the movers, bought food, and made a start on painting. He'd decided on crisp yellow for their living room and a subtle blue in the kitchen; both rooms were half painted. The blue matched the lovely set of expensive dishes Bob's parents had sent them as a housewarming gift, currently spread out all over the counters. Bob stared at them and felt a pang; he had never lived this far from his parents and his childhood home.

Bob poured himself a cup of coffee and stood at the open door to the patio. He peered out at the yard of their new house and inhaled: orange blossoms, sweet and a bit soapy. Freshly cut grass. The drizzle felt peaceful.

He smiled again. He could get used to this, he thought to himself. The air was never sweet in Boston: you were lucky if it didn't carry the smell of car exhaust.

He heard a thump at the front door and realized Marcus must have started delivery of the local newspaper. He opened it as he walked back into the kitchen and was stunned by a huge headline in bold type:

MAYOR'S HUSBAND FOUND DEAD

"Sit," Marcus commanded, carrying the pan of eggs to the table. Bob showed him the headline.

"Jesus," was all Marcus could think to say.

As they ate, Bob read the story out loud. There were few details other than that Mayor Amy Berkman's husband Samuel had been found dead in his office the previous evening. He was apparently due at a dinner in Los Angeles and never made it. Police had not yet said anything about the cause of death, although in a terse statement a spokesperson said foul play could not be ruled out. There were apparently no witnesses; everyone in his office was gone for the day.

Bob put the paper aside and tried to push the murder out of his mind.

Marcus refilled their coffee cups as they discussed what was most important to get done in the house over the weekend. Bob was starting his first real job after law school, as an Assistant District Attorney, and Monday was his official start date. Marcus would be Associate Professor Marcus George at the University of California campus in La Jolla, just north of the city. Classes didn't start until September, but he had an article due and needed to buckle down and finish it.

After breakfast Bob still felt bleary-eyed. He wanted to go back to bed, but he knew they needed to get the house in shape before they both got too busy.

They spent the day unpacking, organizing, painting. Once fully awake Bob hummed early Beatles as he painted, and kept adding to the list of things they needed to do or buy. After a while Marcus found their old records in one of the boxes, and they listened to Ella Fitzgerald and Sarah Vaughn. One of their best memories was a Sarah Vaughn open-air concert in Boston.

When they needed a break they drank iced tea; for lunch they made tuna sandwiches. The rain had stopped and the sun was out; they sat out on the patio at a glass table the previous owners had left behind. Marcus scanned the small garden area.

"Do you have any idea what kind of flowers we can grow here? You grew up in the suburbs, with a yard and garden."

"Wow, flowers," Bob said. "And shrubs and mulch. I guess we really do own a house now. But what to plant? Here? In this climate? No idea."

Marcus laughed. "The American dream. All that's missing is the picket fence."

They went back to unpacking. Bob could feel his jet lag though he tried not to show it; he wanted Marcus to think he was enthusiastic about their new house. He'd thought they should rent for a while, get used to the area, scope out different neighborhoods. But Marcus was ready to buy, and when the University had offered him a really attractive mortgage, with only five percent down, it was too good to pass up.

"Come on, let's buy a house," he had said one early spring evening as they were walking through Harvard Yard, after they had both landed their jobs. "We've joined the Establishment. I'll have tenure. You'll be a lawyer. Let's pretend we're respectable. Two cars, a house, a mortgage, what could be better? We'll worry about crabgrass."

Bob laughed. "I'm not sure they have crabgrass in Southern California."

"So we'll worry about property values and crime. We'll be good upstanding members of the middle class."

Bob could tell Marcus really wanted this. "Okay. But no hot tub. And I absolutely will not be the one to cut the grass."

2

The next morning they were awake by 7:00 a.m. It was drizzling again. They cuddled, and Bob wanted more sleep, but Marcus was energized.

"Up, up, up. There's work to be done."

After their showers Bob went out for lox and bagels and the Sunday *New York Times*. As he waited in line at the little bagel shop, he saw that the Berkman murder had made the front page.

The police announcement simply said that Samuel Berkman had been stabbed and they had no suspects as of yet. Amy Berkman issued a brief statement asking for privacy for her family "at this extraordinarily difficult time." Outside the bagel shop a few people were looking over the newspapers, talking about the murder.

"Poor Amy," someone said as Bob made his way back to his car.

The brand-new gray Honda Civic hatchback was a congratulatory gift from his parents. As his smiling father handed him the keys on the morning of his Harvard graduation, Bob realized his adulthood was smacking him in the face. He had a spouse in all but name, they had bought a house—in California, no less—he had landed a great but undoubtedly demanding job, and now he owned a car. It was all wonderful, the kind of life he wanted, or thought he did, but he had moments, sometimes, when he wondered. He was only 26. Friends he knew from college were still deciding what to do with their lives, taking time to travel or try this job or that, live here or there, experiment. Several were trying to decide if they were gay or bi or straight.

But here he was, settling down to what seemed like a conventional path—albeit the gay version—with all the trappings. It would be a great life, he hoped, and he had known he was gay since he was 11. He loved Marcus deeply, knew how lucky he was to have found him. But sometimes he felt a nagging sense of . . . something, something he couldn't quite name, but whatever it was, the feeling made him uncomfortable.

Bob understood that life meant choices, though he was not quite mature enough to fully accept that choices usually carried loss in their wake.

His train of thought was interrupted as soon as he got home. Marcus had the phone in his hand and handed Bob the receiver. It was the Chief Assistant DA, Duane Houston,

Bob's immediate superior, who had interviewed him several times. They had connected when they talked about Harvard Law, had had some of the same professors, and both had worked on the *Law Review*.

"The boss wants you to shadow me on the Berkman murder, at least until you pass the bar exam. I'm on my way to the crime scene. Meet me there." He gave Bob the address and told him how to find it. "It's right near you. You can dress somewhat casual, it's Sunday. But plan on a long day."

Bob hung up and stared at the telephone receiver. Then he gulped a glass of orange juice, spilling some on his T-shirt. He hurried into the bedroom to change clothes, then back into the kitchen, where Marcus was making coffee and spreading the lox on a plate.

"I have to go to work," he said as he fastened his belt and quickly ate a piece of lox with his fingers. He kissed Marcus on the cheek, grabbed two bagels, and left for his first real day as a lawyer.

Marcus, astonished, stared after him.

3

Sam Berkman's office was in Mission Valley, a nondescript area at the bottom of tall cliffs. Getting there required merging onto a freeway with a steep descent and quickly turning off again. Bob was a nervous driver to begin with, especially when he didn't know his way around. He slowed down a bit to find the right exit and the driver behind him immediately honked, passed him, and gave him the finger as he sped by.

"Welcome to California," Bob muttered to himself.

He looked around as he found his way to the right office building. The Valley was ugly, there was no other word for it. The freeway chopped it in two. Bob had read in a city guidebook that it was a river valley, with the small San Diego River running to the Pacific. The Valley had been the site of the first Spanish building in California in 1769, now long gone. On either side of the freeway lay ugly budget motels and a few office buildings, restaurants, and gyms, including the Holiday Spa, which, he and Marcus had been told, was the gayest gym in town. Behind the buildings the valley gave way on both sides to hills that were mostly rock and dirt, with only a smattering of green. Of course it was early July, and the sun, most days, was blazing. Apparently local vegetation, if it wasn't watered, turned brown in the summer and green in the winter when there was at least a little rain, an inversion Bob knew would take some getting used to.

He had been reading up in preparation for the move. San Diego was essentially in a desert at the edge of the ocean, semi-arid, semi-moist—a climate oddity. Hot sun, most of the time, cooled by ocean breezes, producing what many thought the most perfect climate on earth: temperate, rarely too hot in the summer or too cold in the winter, with a near-constant crispness in the air from the ocean.

But there was little fresh water, and, like Los Angeles, a population center would have been impossible without a vast system of aqueducts built with federal money, carrying water hundreds of miles from the snowy mountains in the north and the Colorado River to the east. Even so, there were regular droughts, and in the summer the tiny San Diego River running through Mission Valley was just a trickle or completely dry.

The more Bob learned about California the stranger it

seemed; he felt as if he had landed on a different planet. It was beautiful, but life could be precarious and danger lurked. He had turned on the radio in the car, and, as he munched on his bagels, the newscaster announced there was a wildfire north of Los Angeles, with evacuations underway.

First weekend, an earthquake and a wildfire, Bob thought to himself. What next, locusts?

As he neared the Berkman office building he saw a few reporters with microphones; uniformed police officers were keeping them away from the building entrance. The building was three stories of glass and steel with stucco trim, with weird protruding smoked-glass windows. A simple sign hung over the front doors: "Professional Building." Bob's stomach tensed up as he drove nearer, and he broke out in a cold sweat.

As he pulled into the parking lot he was stopped by an officer; he explained that he worked for the District Attorney. Luckily the office had sent him a temporary ID card, just a piece of flimsy cardboard without a picture. The officer was skeptical but let Bob pass, and Bob could see in his rearview mirror that the officer was on his walky-talky, no doubt telling people inside to make sure he wasn't an imposter or a reporter. He parked and walked past the reporters, one of whom shoved a microphone in his face.

"Sir, what can you tell us about the investigation?"

Bob ignored him, tried to look business-like, and ducked to get under the yellow crime-scene tape. In the lobby two officers stopped him and looked at his ID. One rode the elevator with him to the third floor and the double doors of the Berkman suite, where Cathy Anderson, the DA's office manager, stood just inside.

"It's all right, officer, he's with us." The cop turned around and left.

"Thanks." Bob told her about the reporter who had asked him a question.

"Yeah, the press lives for this kind of thing. They're hoping for a statement, which they won't get today. When did you arrive?"

"I flew in Friday night."

"Eesh. You must still be a little jet-lagged. And here we've thrown you into the deep end of the pool."

Cathy smiled and shook her head. Bob had liked her as soon as they met during his interviews. She was in her mid-forties with dark hair and blue eyes, a California native, Bob knew, and, he was told, had done a year of law school before deciding it wasn't for her. She was always impeccably dressed, often with a silk scarf around her neck. She wore a wedding ring and had a picture of her family on her desk: her beaming husband, two blond kids, a boy and a girl, and a German shepherd. The husband also had dark black hair— he was from New York—but both kids were fair. Bob tried to work out how that happened.

"Recessive gene," he had shrugged when he told Marcus.

"No, they put blond stuff in the water," Marcus had joked.

Berkman's outer office held two desks, chairs, and a couch. Tasteful prints hung on the walls. Through another pair of double doors Bob could see the crime scene, with a few men walking around in paper booties and rubber gloves. Cathy handed Bob a pair of each.

He could see signs of a struggle—an overturned chair, what looked to be a broken glass on the floor, a file cabinet open with files pulled halfway out. There was a large bloodstain on the gray carpet, and, just like on TV, the shape of the corpse on the floor outlined in white chalk. The body had been removed and was presumably at the coroner's office.

Duane Houston came out to greet him. His boss was a wholesomely handsome man with brown hair, green eyes, and a chiseled face. He wore aviator glasses and was always fiddling with them, taking them off, putting them back on or polishing them with a handkerchief. He did it so often everyone wondered if the glasses were a prop, meant to make him look like a formidable attorney. Seeing him on the street you might easily assume he was a male model or an actor, a bland California male, a common representative of the local species.

"Sorry to drag you in on a Sunday, but this case is going to be massive."

Bob nodded.

I'm going to need help." Duane lowered his voice. "The office is short-handed, there's been a lot of turnover with people leaving. Mostly for more money. We're hiring, but right now there's no one else, everyone else has their hands full."

"I understand." Bob was an employee now, he suddenly realized. He would do as he was told.

"There was a struggle, although it's possible it was staged," Duane went on. "There was no sign of forced entry, either to the building or the office, but there's no security, so it's not clear if Berkman knew his assailant. The outside door wasn't locked up until later in the evening. The ME's guess is time of death is around six or seven p.m., but she'll know more after the autopsy."

They both stared at the bloodstain on the floor.

"There's not much to go on so far," Duane said, letting out a deep breath.

Bob asked who found the body.

"The cleaning crew, around ten on Friday evening. Apparently the office staff always left the door to the office open until the cleaning crew arrived, and they normally locked it when they left."

They moved into the large inner office, where Duane guided him around the chalk toward the large desk at the opposite end of the room and introduced Bob to two detectives.

The older, Richard Perez, was going through the desk drawers, and the other, Gus Bobbitt, was looking through a file cabinet. They were both wearing rumpled dark blue suits and almost identical red ties; they reminded Bob of old movie characters. Looking at Perez he thought of Dana Andrews's no-nonsense detective in Otto Preminger's *Laura*; Bobbitt looked like the veteran character actor Jack Palance.

Bob smiled to himself. Ever since he had written his senior honors thesis at Brown on Southern women in film, he thought of almost everyone he met in movie terms. He had thought of Marcus as a young John Garfield the moment he met him.

The detectives nodded and continued their search. Perez had what looked like a perpetual scowl on his face and Bob's stomach tensed again. They looked hard-boiled, straight out of Dashiell Hammett novels, though Bob later learned that both had been born in the Midwest, enlisted in the Marines, were stationed in San Diego, and decided to stay.

"I want you to see the note." Duane guided Bob over to the front of the large desk.

On the side of the desk blotter was a piece of scratch paper. Even upside down, Bob could see that it said simply "A @ 5."

"The boss"—by which Duane meant Fred Stevens, the District Attorney—"talked to the mayor briefly yesterday. She confirmed that Berkman was due home around then.

The plan was they would have an early dinner with their kids and then drive to LA for a reception."

Bob nodded.

"He never made it home, so Amy assumed he was held up. She called here but there was no answer. Then she summoned her driver and went to LA by herself. The driver confirms. Apparently she didn't want to miss the event, and it seems Sam was often held up. She didn't think anything bad had happened until later, when she got home."

Bob nodded again. He stared at the note for a while. "A @ 5."

"There were fingerprints on pieces of that glass." Duane pointed to the remnants of glass on the carpet. "So far no match to anyone, but we're still checking. There were also prints on that one." Duane pointed to a used crystal glass on a silver tray sitting on a credenza against the wall. Next to it were more glasses and two expensive-looking decanters. One was filled with amber liquid, the other with something thicker with a slightly lighter color.

Perez spoke up for the first time, in an unexpectedly deep voice. "We spoke to Berkman's secretary, a Ms. Russo. Berkman had one meeting Friday afternoon, with one of his investors. And he met someone for lunch, but she didn't know who, didn't know if it was business related. We didn't get much from her, she was pretty shaken up and her doctor had given her a sedative."

"Scotch and brandy, I assume," Bob guessed, looking at the credenza.

"Right, we'll test them." Perez returned to the desk drawers. It seemed he wasn't finding anything unusual. Bobbitt had not even looked up while his partner was speaking, just continued placing manila folders on top of one of the filing cabinets.

Duane looked at his watch. "We need to get to the office to meet with the boss. Then the medical examiner should be ready for us. Perez, you can meet us at the morgue."

In the parking lot, Duane took off his glasses and told Bob the best way to drive to the DA's downtown office. The sun was out now and it was getting warm, although not humid. Bob felt a trickle of sweat under his arms and reminded himself to bring sunglasses. And maybe he needed a linen jacket; his East coast wool was clearly not going to work, at least not in the California summer.

4

The office was in the central courthouse in downtown San Diego, a somewhat decrepit Spanish-style building in an old, sketchy section of town. The city had expanded outward from the central hub, and in the nineteenth century the original core held some large mansions as well as saloons and hotels. In fact, Bob remembered from his reading, San Diego was the first terminus of the transcontinental railroad, which arrived during the Civil War and produced the first of several real estate booms.

The mansions of that era were now long gone, and most blocks were filled with ordinary buildings, offices, shops, and restaurants. The only people on the street seemed to be the homeless, but of course, Bob realized, it was Sunday. Office workers wouldn't be around. Not that there was much walking in San Diego: even on a busy weekday people drove everywhere. The joke was that you knew you were a real Southern Californian when you found yourself driving from one end of a shopping mall to the other.

Bob knew from his reading that there had been a fair number of downtown-centered scandals over the years, some involving a corrupt police force, including bootlegging in the 1920s and gambling in the 1930s. He couldn't quite recall all the details, but he vaguely remembered a disgraced mayor who ran away, or was run out of town. The military always had a huge presence; San Diego provided a natural harbor, like San Francisco. There had always been marines and sailors everywhere; downtown was full of places that catered to them, from bars and tattoo parlors to cheap hotels, where the rooms, like the hookers, rented by the hour.

Bob parked in a garage down the block. Cathy was waiting for him in the lobby and introduced him to the guard on duty. Bob noticed that he carried a gun. In the elevator on the way to Duane's seventh-floor office Cathy assured Bob she'd get him a photo ID by the next day.

The hallway lights hadn't been turned on, and the only light was from a dirty window at the end of the hall. Bob smelled dust and floor wax. Duane's office was large, with an old wooden desk, filing cabinets, and a conference table. There was a map of California on the wall. Duane stood up, buttoned his coat, and said, "Let's go, he's waiting." Cathy went into her office adjoining Duane's.

As Duane and Bob walked down the dark hall a man approached from the other direction and stopped.

Duane stopped. "Sandy, I'm so sorry. This must be awful for you, and for Amy and the kids."

The man nodded. He was short with brown hair and blue eyes and looked tired. Bob guessed he was around forty; he looked a bit like Jack Nicholson. There was something else striking about him but Bob couldn't quite figure out what.

"Bob, this is Sandy Nelson, the mayor's chief of staff."

They shook hands and Nelson gave a slight, crooked smile. Bob wasn't sure, but his gaydar picked up at least a little gay vibration.

When Bob first heard the term "gaydar" he was skeptical that such a thing existed, but as time went on, he realized there really was something to it, something about the gay demeanor. Or maybe it was pheromones.

Duane asked Nelson how the mayor was doing.

"I haven't seen her. I just flew in from Phoenix, I was visiting my sister. I was there when I got the news."

There was an awkward silence.

"We'll be in touch," Nelson said. He seemed in a hurry to get away, and continued walking toward the elevators.

Bob realized the mayor's chief of staff must have been talking to the DA, and wondered why that was happening so soon after the murder. Even if nothing untoward was going on, didn't it give the appearance of political interference?

Maybe that was why Nelson was so abrupt, Bob thought; he might have been embarrassed about being there at all. He glanced at his boss, hoping he would explain or comment, but Duane said nothing. Bob opened his mouth to voice concern, but stopped himself.

The office of District Attorney Fred Stevens, whom Bob had met only briefly, was large and elegantly furnished. They walked through a large outer office to the inner sanctum, which held a huge desk, a couch, lots of bookshelves filled with legal tomes, and a beautiful polished wood conference table. The DA was in his early forties and had made a name for himself as an attorney representing local residents, often Latino, in lawsuits against the police department and, in a few prominent cases, against federal officials dealing with the

Mexican border, only fifteen miles south of downtown. A San Diego native, he had attended Berkeley and Stanford Law, and had deep California roots. Everyone described him as a no-nonsense, straightforward lawyer, and a very ambitious one.

Stevens was seated at the conference table. A large man in a police uniform faced him. "Perez is the best we have," he was saying. Stevens nodded, then stood and shook Bob's hand.

"Bob. This is Jerry Murphy, our chief of police."

Murphy shook Bob's hand without getting up. He was a large man, maybe 250 pounds. *Maybe that's why he stayed seated*, Bob thought. The DA motioned for Bob and Duane to take seats. There was a pitcher of water and glasses in the center of the table.

Chief Murphy spoke. "I'll let you guys get on with it. Duane, the ME is ready for you as soon as you're done here. Perez and Bobbitt are on their way."

He stood up quickly and left. Bob was surprised at how easily he got out of his chair; he carried his weight well. Stevens got up to shut the door after him, retrieved a file from his desk, and sat down again. He opened the file and spent a moment looking over the top page. He had a habit of opening and closing his left hand into a fist as he read.

"Okay. Bob, I know you just arrived, and you need to study for the bar, but we are short-handed right now."

Bob nodded. "Yes, sir. Duane explained the situation."

"I want you to follow Duane's lead on everything. Both of you need to keep your eyes on the police investigation. I don't have to tell you, this is a high-profile case. The press, not just local, is going to be all over us. I want at least one of you there when the police question every major witness, and watching through the glass for interviews with suspects. The cops need to dot every *i* and cross every *t*. Absolutely no funny business."

Bob had watched enough cop shows on TV to know that being constantly observed by the DA's office would not go down well with the police. Stevens saw the look of concern on his face.

"I know. It's not the usual thing. But nothing here will be. I've cleared this with Chief Murphy, and he will clear it with his people. I have his word. Any detective or cop who doesn't like it, you tell me, and he's off the case. Any questions?" Stevens was once again opening and closing the fingers of his left hand.

Duane spoke up. "Have they questioned anyone yet?"

"Except for a very brief conversation with Sam's secretary to determine what his schedule was, no. That will all start tomorrow. The Mayor is off limits for a week, she's observing Jewish . . ." He searched for the word.

"Shiva," Bob said. "The traditional period of mourning."

"Right. Shiva. Thank you."

"I don't understand," Duane blurted out. "Amy isn't Jewish herself—"

The DA cut him off. "She's doing it to honor her husband. And for Sam's relatives, some of whom live here, and up and down the coast, and will visit. Is that so hard to understand?"

And, Bob thought to himself, Mayor Amy doesn't want to appear callous; that wouldn't play with the voters. He was a bit shocked by his own cynicism.

He looked over to Duane, who had turned bright red and taken off his glasses.

The DA continued. "Chief Murphy and I will hold a press conference tomorrow afternoon. There won't be any real news but we need to feed the vultures something. Assure the public we're on the case."

"What about the funeral?" Bob asked. "A Jewish funeral is usually quick."

"Right. Sam will be buried tomorrow in his family's plot in San Francisco. We've already alerted the SF department to keep the press away as best they can. They will have security there, I hope at a discreet distance, but of course it's out in the open, so who knows. It could be a zoo. Someone will take photos, so we'll know who was there. It will be a brief graveside service with just family and a few close friends. The family will fly up there as soon as we release the body. The White House is providing a plane." For a moment the DA looked truly sad. He stopped opening and closing his left fist.

Duane raised his eyebrows. "The White House?"

Fred cleared his throat. "Well, they see Amy as a rising star in the party. Someone with national presence. I imagine the RNC is actually paying for it."

Duane looked skeptical; he was about to say more when Fred cut him off.

"I think that's everything," Fred quickly said. "Get down to the morgue. Keep me informed."

Bob and Duane stood to leave.

"And Bob, welcome." Stevens went back to his desk.

As they left the office, Bob wondered what the hell he was doing in the middle of a case involving the White House.

He was feeling a kind of vertigo. Just three days ago he had been packing suitcases 3,000 miles away, saying good-bye to friends, walking through Harvard Square. He had been told he'd have a relatively easy month or two, studying for the bar exam, learning his way around. Yet here he was in the middle of a sensational murder.

Too much, too fast.

He told himself to concentrate on today, as his mother

used to tell him whenever he felt overwhelmed. Thinking of his Jewish mother made him think about food, and he realized he was starving. He didn't think looking at a dead body on an empty stomach was a great idea, but he dutifully followed Duane to the elevator.

Duane pressed "B."

5

The basement morgue smelled of chemicals and felt musty. The fluorescent lights buzzed. Duane guided Bob to an anteroom, where the Medical Examiner, Melinda Ivanov, came out and met them. Duane introduced Bob and she smiled and nodded. Melinda was wearing a blue gown, a hairnet, and rubber gloves. She looked to be around fifty and wore no makeup.

Duane walked over to a counter, lit a cigarette, and offered one to Bob. "You might want this. Supposed to help with the smell."

Bob smiled and shook his head no.

"Okay," Duane said. "But if you faint, don't blame me."

The ME motioned to a tall cabinet, and Duane and Bob put on blue gowns and booties. Melinda brought them into her workroom, where Perez and Bobbitt—Dana Andrews and Jack Palance, Bob thought—were gowned and waiting. They were smoking. The room held stainless steel sinks, counters, and a lot of medical equipment.

The body of Sam Berkman lay on a stainless steel slab in the middle of the room. A sheet covered him to his neck. From his face, Bob guessed his age to be about fifty. He had regular features and a full head of black hair mixed with some gray. His eyes were closed.

"He was stabbed seven times," the ME began, indicating the torso with a blue-gloved hand. "The cause of death was hypovolemic shock from loss of blood. Death would have been relatively quick, within a few minutes, but he did bleed out quite a bit."

She lifted the sheet. The knife wounds were visible on the chest and on both arms, and there was a large incision in the shape of a Y, which, Bob assumed, allowed the ME to do the autopsy. At the sight of the incisions and the wounds, Bob felt dizzy; he closed his eyes for a moment. The smell of blood was overpowering.

"The murder weapon was a small or medium-sized knife with a serrated edge, something like a hunting knife or an ordinary bread knife or steak knife. The wounds were deep. There is evidence of a struggle, broken nails and a broken finger on his right hand." Melinda lifted the arm to show them. "I would surmise the victim tried to fight off the assailant, who was right-handed and strong. I'd say you're probably looking for a male."

At the mention of a struggle, Duane's expression changed from neutral to something else, Bob thought. Shock, perhaps, or resignation.

"Based on the usual factors, I put time of death between six and eight p.m."

Perez spoke for the first time. He fiddled with his red tie. "Can you narrow that down at all?"

"Sorry, no. One more thing. The victim had within the previous twenty-four hours. Or perhaps say, had ejaculated. His clothes revealed no clue assailant's identity."

Melinda paused. "Any questions?"

Duane and Perez both shook their heads. Duane spoke. "None I can think of now. Is the body ready to be released to the family?"

"Yes. Someone from the mayor's office dropped off some clean clothes." Bob assumed that was the mayor's Chief of Staff, Sandy Nelson.

Dr. Ivanov's manner became slightly less formal. "We'll dress him and I'll call the number I was given. A coffin is already here. I'll type up my report and get copies to you."

They were all silent for a moment, maybe out of respect, or simply habit. Then she looked at Bob, who was staring intently at the face of the dead man. "Young man, I suggest you get some fresh air as soon as possible. It's been a long time since I've seen anyone turn that particular shade of green."

6

The four men got into the elevator and Duane pushed "1." He turned to Bob. "Get some air, then come up to my office." Bobbitt smirked.

Bob and the officers got off in the lobby. The three of them walked outside, and Perez said, "See you, kid," as they left him on the sidewalk.

Bob inhaled and looked up at the sky. It was now around 80 degrees, with a cool breeze coming off the ocean. He couldn't get the sight of Sam Berkman's lifeless face out of his brain.

The guard came out and asked if he was all right. "Your
"

"Yes. Is it that obvious?"

"It's never easy, but they say the first is always the worst." He briefly put his arm on Bob's shoulder and then went back to his desk in the lobby.

Bob looked at his watch: 1:30. It felt much later than that. He went back in and took the elevator to Duane's office. Cathy was there and they were eating sandwiches.

"Eat something," Cathy said. "It will help. I remembered from your interview, you like tuna fish. There are some drinks in the little fridge."

Bob thanked her, grabbed a can of ginger ale, which he hoped would settle his stomach, and joined them at the conference table. For a few minutes, they sat quietly and ate. The food did help; Bob felt his pulse returning to normal.

Finally Duane spoke. He took off his glasses and nervously polished them. The room felt uncomfortable; Bob realized that the murder victim was someone they knew, someone at least peripherally in their own circle, the professional, political, legal world. Suddenly Duane put down his glasses.

"All right. So there's no question that this is a vicious murder. The perp was angry. So we need to start looking into Sam's life. Are there any skeletons? Enemies?"

"Could it have been a stranger, a thief?" Cathy asked.

"Doesn't feel like it," Duane said. "Not with seven deep stab wounds. This was personal. And what was there to steal? There wasn't even a safe in the office."

Of course, Bob thought, someone might not have known that, or could have been there to steal a file, but he didn't say anything.

"Bob, tomorrow we'll stick with the detectives as they start interviews. And I need you to start going through Sam's financial records, see if anything looks funny. The detectives brought some files, they're in your office, you can start now. One of them is his will; start there. We'll bring in a forensic accountant but in the meantime, you can see if anything sticks out."

"I have an office?" Bob asked.

"Yes, you're a big boy now," Cathy said with a friendly smile. "Come on, I'll show you."

Duane added, "And just in case you were wondering, we wear long pants every weekday."

They laughed, and the tension dissipated.

Bob thought for a moment. "What about the mayor? Could this have been related to her? Someone angry at her? Or trying to derail her career? I hear she's pretty ambitious. Or could there be an anti-Semitic angle?"

Cathy looked down.

Duane looked uncomfortable. "Yes, I suppose it could be aimed at Amy. Although it doesn't seem likely, at least not at this point. For one thing, this will gain her a great deal of public sympathy. It's a horrible way to get it, but it will probably boost her career, not hurt it."

Bob hadn't thought of that, but it made sense. A new thought was forming in his mind but he couldn't quite grab it.

Duane went on. "And the anti-Jewish angle? I doubt it. If bigots were looking to make a point, why not leave some sign? And no hate group has claimed responsibility or anything like that. Usually that happens within twenty-four hours."

"What about Sam?" Cathy asked. "Do we have any sense of who might want to do this?"

Duane got up to fetch another drink from the little fridge. "Well, we know he was a big-shot property developer, all up and down the coast. And very rich. We'll have to look into the nuts and bolts. Follow the money. Apparently he had some financial ties to Keating and Lincoln Savings, but national and local reporters are all over that story—and no accusations have been made against Sam."

Lincoln Savings had been in the national news for months. A savings and loan bank in Irvine, roughly halfway between San Diego and Los Angeles, it was at the center of the scandal that would almost certainly end up costing the taxpayers billions. Charles Keating had taken over Lincoln a few years before, fired existing management, and made highly risky investments, thanks to the free-market mania and push for deregulation that had swept through Congress during the Reagan years.

Bob also remembered reading that Keating apparently believed that some of the bank regulators were "homos" who were against him because of his moral outlook. He had looked to Washington politicians for help and made large contributions to many of them, including Alan Cranston, Democratic Senator of California. There was a general sense that the scandal might mean the end of Cranston's long career.

Great, Bob said to himself. *A dead body and a national political scandal.*

The meeting ended, and Cathy showed Bob to his office, one floor below. It was a small room painted an ugly beige, with an old wooden desk, two beat-up filing cabinets, and some chairs. A phone had already been installed. A stack of files was sitting in the middle of the desk.

"Let me know if you need anything. I put office supplies in the drawer. Your computer should be here tomorrow or Tuesday. We have a guy, he'll set it up. There's a bit of a budget for furniture, you can spruce it up if you like, some lamps, a few prints for the walls, maybe a rug."

Bob thanked her and sat behind the desk. The chair was

uncomfortable and squeaked. The window looked out on a parking lot and, Bob realized, faced north, so the room wouldn't get a lot of light.

He stared at the pile of files and sighed.

7

Bob picked up his phone and called Marcus, who answered after two rings.

"Can we go back to Boston?"

Marcus laughed. "It's that bad?"

"Well," Bob sighed. "I'm working on the murder of the mayor's husband. I saw the crime scene and I attended the autopsy. No question, it was murder. Bloody. Awful. I met two hard-boiled detectives who are straight out of Hollywood, and the Irish chief of police, also from central casting."

"Jesus. When will you be home?"

"In a couple of hours. I have stuff to do."

"We'll go out to dinner. I'm almost finished painting the kitchen, and all the kitchen stuff has been put away. I even put in shelf paper. Just call me Donna Reed, happy housewife."

Bob laughed. Of the two of them, it was usually Bob who had been more domestic. Until now. "See you later, Donna. Meet me at the door with a martini."

The file on top of the pile on his desk was marked "SB Will." Bob opened it and read. It seemed straightforward, with trust funds for the children, real and personal property and bank and investment accounts to his wife, with several accounts already jointly owned and therefore requiring no transfer. There were a few bequests of personal items to other family members and individuals labeled "my friend so-and-so."

Only one thing caught Bob's eye, a bequest of $20,000, with no explanation, to a Gerald Otley of New York City. He was the only person not labeled a friend or relative. Bob made a note to ask Duane if the name meant anything to him.

Bob set the will aside. The rest of the files were labeled with the names of building projects along with dates; he assumed that Bobbitt had pulled anything that looked current. The project names were the usual run of real-estate broker-babble—Sierra Vista, Carmel Valley Heights. There were notes about budgets that Bob didn't know how to interpret, geological notes about building sites, and loan documents from various banks, including Keating's bank. The sums involving Lincoln Savings seemed rather large to Bob, but he didn't know enough about these kinds of projects to know if anything he saw was suspicious. He hoped the forensic accountant could sort it out for him.

One note in one file, about a project in Oceanside north of San Diego, did raise Bob's eyebrows. It was handwritten on Lincoln Savings stationery, thanking Sam for "coming up with a plan that allowed us an equity position." He took the elevator up to the seventh floor to show it to Duane, but Cathy said he had just left. She was gathering her things.

"Can it keep until tomorrow?" she asked while she adjusted her silk scarf.

"Yes, of course."

"Duane said to tell you to meet him here at eight."

"Okay, no problem."

She handed him a business card. "Here's my card. I've

put my home number on the back. Let me know if anything comes up that can't wait."

Bob thanked her.

"Relax tonight. You're still looking a little green."

8

B ob went down to his office for his coat. He looked at his watch; it was after 5:00. He suddenly realized he was exhausted. On the drive home he listened to a local news station; the Berkman murder was still the lead story. He changed the station to one playing the Beach Boys.

Marcus met him at the front door and did his best Barbra Streisand imitation, which wasn't very good but always made Bob laugh. "Oy, what a day I had today." It was a favorite line from *Funny Girl*.

He handed Bob the martini he had asked for. Bob drank it down in two large gulps.

"It was that bad?"

"Exhausting. And upsetting. And complicated. Other than that, it was great." Bob collapsed on the couch.

Marcus chuckled. "Well, cheer up. Take a shower. I'm taking you out to a fancy dinner. We have a seven-thirty reservation."

As Bob started for the bedroom, the front doorbell rang.

"Who could that be?" Marcus asked, following Bob to the door.

On their front stoop stood Bob's brother and sister-in-law, Alex and Carol, who lived in Los Angeles. They were both smiling widely and carrying baskets of food and wine.

"Surprise!" Carol said as she kissed both of them on the cheek. Alex hugged his brother and gave Marcus a friendly punch in the arm. Bob was smiling ear to ear while Marcus quickly excused himself to cancel their dinner reservation.

It was easy to tell that Alex and Bob were brothers, Marcus always thought: they had the same build, the same hair, almost the exact same face, except that Alex had their father's nose and Bob their mother's. Carol, Bob told Marcus, looked like a Jewish Diane Keaton.

Los Angeles was about a two-hour drive up the freeway, and the nearness of Alex and Carol had helped them decide San Diego could be a good fit. They had gone through several anxious months of applying for their jobs and waiting to see if they both could land them, and by some miracle, it worked—two jobs in the same city. They knew they were beating the odds: most couples with one (or, God forbid, two) professionals had to settle for living separately and commuting, which seldom worked over the long run. Marcus knew several academic couples who had broken up after trying to commute. Bob had turned down a clerkship with a federal judge to take the ADA job, but he hadn't hesitated: he'd known it was the right thing to do.

Marcus had met his in-laws a few times when they visited Bob's family home in Connecticut. Alex was five years the elder, an attorney like their father. Now Bob had followed the same path. Carol was a freelance illustrator for children's books as well as an aspiring novelist. They had a young son, named Jacob after his grandfather; they called him Jay. Marcus and Bob had gone to Danbury for the boy's bris, which Bob called "the traditional ritual mutilation."

Neither of them had ever been to such an event, except their own, of course. Marcus nearly fainted.

Alex and Carol had left Jay with a neighbor for the evening, along with their golden retriever. The boy and the dog were inseparable, according to Carol. When Jay had started pre-school Sophie would sit by the front door waiting for him to come home, looking forlorn and gently whimpering. Carol, who worked from home, said it drove her crazy.

It was a lovely evening with a gentle breeze, not warm, not cold. Perfect. They ate outside using their new blue dishes and talked about Sam Berkman's death.

Bob knew Alex was getting involved in local politics, even toying with the idea of running for office himself some day. It turned out Alex knew the Berkmans slightly; in fact, he and Carol had just seen Amy at the dinner in Los Angeles that she had attended on the night of Sam's murder. They had wondered why Sam wasn't there; he was almost always at her side at events like that.

Alex explained that Mayor Amy, a nominal Republican, was highly ambitious and was planning to run for higher office, aiming perhaps at the Governor's mansion or the Senate, while Sam, the real estate developer with projects up and down the coast, was a nominal Democrat.

"Nominal?" Marcus asked.

"The Berkman's are an old, distinguished Democratic family. I don't think he cared about politics one way or another. His thing is money, not politics."

"And Amy?" Bob asked.

"She's an old-fashioned Republican. Fiscally conservative, socially moderate, like the old Northeast Republicans. But it's getting harder for her and people like her, the party is changing, becoming much more conservative. Everything changed with Reagan. The evangelical vote is now the Republican base. But so far Amy has been able to finesse things."

"And are you a nominal Democrat?" Bob teased. Bob considered himself a liberal Democrat and knew that Alex tended to be more of a centrist.

"If I run for office, I will be."

Everyone laughed.

"I didn't know him at all well, but I can't imagine Sam mixed up in anything shady," Alex continued. "And he was in good health, I'm sure. There must have been foul play. Must have been. A thief, maybe."

Bob didn't say anything about the investigation; he didn't know if he could, or if he could even say if he was working on the case. The job was so new to him he didn't know the rules for situations like this.

His brother could see talk of death was casting a pall. "Sophie is pregnant," he triumphantly announced. "You'll have to take one of the puppies."

They had decided to breed Sophie to give her puppies to look after, at least for a while, so she'd stop missing Jay so much during the day. Bob was thrilled; Marcus was less sure but said nothing.

"Oh, wonderful! Give us one of the boys," Bob said. "We'll name him Oscar. For Oscar Wilde. We'll get one of those baby gates and keep him in that little alcove off the kitchen. We'll put up a fence in the back yard."

Marcus knew Bob well enough to know that he had made up his mind. He was doing that a lot lately, Marcus realized, making quick decisions.

Bob was coming into his own, he thought. Finishing law school with honors, editing the *Law Review*, landing a plum job with the district attorney. Marcus was happy for him, and proud, but could also detect some subtle shifts in him. He wasn't the same impressionable student just out of college he had been when they first got together four years before. At times while Bob was in law school, always studying late into the night, Marcus had felt more alone than he had before they met. When he felt that way, he told himself he was being silly, but now he wondered if that sense of aloneness might return.

Alex mentioned that there was a fundraiser coming up soon in Rancho Santa Fe for the ACLU and said he would send them an invitation.

"You should come. Lots of folks you should meet will be there."

"We'll be there, for sure," Bob said. North of San Diego, Rancho Santa Fe was one of the wealthiest enclaves in the country, full of beautiful, large estates.

They lingered over a homemade cheesecake as it got dark and a bit chilly.

"My God, this is delicious," Marcus said to Carol. "Did you really make this yourself?"

"Oh, it's easy. Really."

Although he could handle simple things like eggs, nothing in the kitchen seemed easy to Marcus. He liked to joke that it was not the room of the house in which he excelled, which always made Bob smirk. Once in Cambridge for Bob's birthday Marcus had tried to prepare an elaborate meal out of Julia Child, and Bob came home to find their kitchen a wreck and Marcus sweating and swearing as he tried to make roast duck a l'orange. Sauce was everywhere, including the ceiling.

Alex and Carol offered to help with the dishes, but Bob brushed them away, reminding them that they had a long drive home. Alex extracted a promise that they would visit soon.

"Jay keeps asking about Uncle Bob and Uncle Marcus."

They both stopped moving, just for a moment, then smiled at each other. Marcus felt a tear welling up, which he did his best to hide. It was such a little thing, really; Alex and Carol told their son that they had not one but two uncles in San Diego, Uncle Bob and Uncle Marcus.

How much a word could change the world, Marcus thought to himself. Maybe gay life really will be different as the awful 1980s draw to a close, he thought, despite AIDS, despite Reagan, despite everything.

"We'll come to LA soon," Bob promised. "We'll have to see the puppies!"

They did the dishes and Bob was ready for sleep, even though it was only 9:30. "Jet lag," he said. He kissed Marcus, took a shower, and collapsed.

Marcus stayed up for a while, putting books on shelves, then joined Bob in bed, wrapping himself around him.

"What did you say your name was," Bob murmured through a haze of sleep.

"Very funny."

We'll be happy here, Bob thought as he drifted off again. Happy and peaceful in sunny California, just like we planned. Even with earthquakes.

Marcus was thinking the same thing as he inhaled deeply. He loved the way Bob smelled.

A few weeks later, they remembered that night and laughed. By then Bob was deep into the investigation of the mayor's dead husband.

9

The next morning Bob woke with the alarm at 6:30, and Marcus groaned and turned over.

"Couldn't you have found a job that starts at a civilized hour? Like noon?"

Bob smiled and kissed his shoulder.

He showered, dressed in a suit and tie, and gulped down some orange juice and a leftover bagel. He made it to the office at a few minutes past 8:00. He noticed morning rush hour traffic was heavy and made a mental note to adjust travel times on weekdays. The sun had already burned through the haze and it was going to be a warm day.

The same guard was on duty when Bob entered the office building. He flashed a big smile and Bob waved back, and began to wonder if the guard might be gay. Bob knew his own persona sent gay men's gaydar into the red zone, although he never could quite figure out why.

He joined Cathy and Duane in Duane's office.

"Morning," Duane said with too much cheeriness for that time in the morning. "I hope yesterday wasn't too traumatic for you." He motioned to a coffee pot.

Bob poured a cup. "No, though clearly autopsies take some getting used to."

"Well normally, we don't go to those. But on this case, we need to watch everything."

Bob took his seat. "Right."

"So here's the plan. This morning the detectives will start interviewing Sam Berkman's staff. There were two secretaries in the office. They'll start there. You'll sit in. You're there to observe. If you notice something they overlook, let them know, or let me know, depending on what it is. If there's a question that you think really needs to be asked that they don't ask, ask it. All clear?"

"Yes, no problem."

"Good. Their first interview is at nine-fifteen with the

executive secretary at Berkman's office. Meet the detectives in the parking lot or the lobby and go up together. She knows you're coming. Meanwhile, the forensic accountant will be in this morning and will start going through Sam's finances."

Duane paused. "Did you see anything in those files?"

"The will is straightforward, but there were two things I noticed."

"Oh?" There was a touch of worry in Duane's voice. He was polishing his glasses.

"Yes. The first is a handwritten note from Charles Keating that suggests deep financial involvement and a personal relationship."

Both Duane and Cathy sat back in their chairs. Cathy closed her eyes for a moment.

Bob waited for them to say something in response, but they didn't, so he continued. "The other is a bequest in the will to a Gerald Otley in New York. Everyone else in the will is labeled a friend or whatever—cousin, nephew—but Otley isn't identified. Does the name ring any bell?"

"Gerald Otley. I don't think so. See what you can find out about him when you have a minute. And Keating, that's . . . interesting. Of course whatever business they did together could have been totally legit. Lincoln Savings invested in projects all over California."

"Still, I assume the accountant should look at the relationship carefully."

Duane cleared his throat. "Yes, of course. Cathy, make me a copy of the note. Two copies, we should also show it to the boss." Duane looked at his watch. "You'd better get going."

Cathy followed Bob down to his office to retrieve the note.

"How's your house coming along? Any buyer's remorse?"

Bob smiled. "No, not yet. Marcus is getting the place in shape."

At his first interview Bob had been sure to mention Marcus to see if he would pick up any hint of homophobia; it pleasantly surprised him that there was none. But Cathy's question made him feel a pang of guilt for not being there to help more with the house, though he was sure Marcus understood. Or hoped he did.

The IT specialist was setting up the new Macintosh in Bob's office; Bob got a quick overview and then left for Berkman's office, steeling himself for meeting the two detectives again. He was beginning to think of them as Frick and Frack; he just hoped they wouldn't keep calling him "kid."

10

Bob pulled into the Mission Valley parking lot. It was full of cars, unlike yesterday. The reporters were gone and there was only one policeman standing at the entrance.

A few minutes later the detectives pulled up in a Buick.

"Morning, kid. You know the drill?" said Perez, the older detective.

"I do."

"We ask the questions, you listen."

Bob pretended he didn't hear that. "I've been going through the files you pulled from the office. We"—Bob emphasized the word—"need to ask them about Berkman's relationship to Lincoln Savings and Charles Keating. There's evidence in the files of a close relationship."

Perez grunted. Bob wondered if all detectives in

California were required to watch Humphrey Bogart movies as part of their training.

Berkman's executive secretary, Florence Russo, met them at the office door and immediately offered coffee, which all three accepted. She was an attractive woman of around forty wearing a dark gray suit and high heels. She had been crying.

When they settled in, Perez and Bobbitt took out notebooks and Perez began with the obvious questions—how long had she worked for Berkman, what were her duties.

"Can you think of anyone who might wish Mr. Berkman harm? Did he have enemies?"

Florence Russo hesitated. "I can't think of anyone who would do this to him, no."

Bob noticed that Russo hadn't exactly answered the precise questions.

Perez continued. "Earlier that day, he met with James Cunningham, one of his business partners."

"Yes."

"What was the nature of their relationship?"

"Mr. Cunningham invested in some of Mr. Berkman's real estate projects. I believe they were meeting to discuss their most recent project."

Bob spoke up. "If I may."

Perez looked annoyed, but Bob ignored him. "What was the source of the funds Mr. Cunningham invested?" Bob remembered references to "JC" in some of the files that also held references to Lincoln Savings.

Russo took a sip of her coffee. "I believe they were personal funds. Mr. Cunningham is a member of the Los Angeles Cunningham family, and they have substantial personal wealth."

Perez and Bobbitt both looked impressed. Even Bob had heard of the Cunninghams, one of the wealthiest families in

California—and the entire country. The patriarch had been a newspaper publisher who amassed one of the largest real estate empires in the state, and two generations of descendants were prominent in both social and philanthropic circles.

Perez prodded further—how long had Cunningham and Berkman worked together, how much was invested, were they on good terms. Russo said she couldn't comment on amounts or the details of the investments, but she knew they had worked together for at least five years, since she had first come to work for Berkman.

It was Bobbitt's turn to probe for details about the day of the murder. Russo told the men that Berkman had come to the office after lunch, as usual, made a phone call, and met with Cunningham at 2:00 p.m. He then suggested she and her assistant leave early, around 4:00, wishing them a pleasant weekend.

"Did he often suggest you leave that early?'

"Sometimes, yes. He was a kind man." She smiled thinly. Altogether, she told them, it was a routine day in the office, as far as she was aware.

"And you don't know who he was meeting for lunch?"

"No, I'm sorry. I don't. He didn't say anything about it."

The detectives closed their notebooks; then Bob spoke up again and Perez gave him a warning look, which Bob again ignored.

"Mr. Berkman left a note for himself about meeting his wife at five. Do you know, did he often write himself reminder notes such as that? Was that his usual practice?"

Russo thought for a moment. "I couldn't say. He never did want to keep a formal calendar, his schedule was quite loose, so I'm not surprised he'd leave himself a note. But I couldn't really say."

Bob was getting a bit annoyed with Florence Russo; for an executive secretary, she didn't seem to know much.

"And what do you know about the relationship between Mr. Berkman and Lincoln Savings?"

She blanched. "I only know they invested together. Sometimes more, sometimes less."

Perez shot Bob a dirty look. "Well, if there are no other questions, thank you for your time. I believe your colleague is due to speak to us soon."

"Yes. Susan." Russo looked at her watch. "She'll be here soon. Help yourself to more coffee. I'm going to excuse myself; the mayor is expecting me at the house."

Everyone stood up, and Russo quickly took her purse from the top of her desk and left.

Perez turned to Bob. "Kid, we ask, you listen. Is that in any way unclear?"

Bob struggled to stay calm. "It's clear. But those aren't my instructions. I work for the District Attorney, not for you or your department. If you have a problem, take it up with your superiors." If Perez is going to play Humphrey Bogart, Bob thought to himself, I'll play Claude Rains. Sooner or later he'll realize I'm a good guy, and we'll walk off together, just like in *Casablanca*.

Or not.

Perez glared and fiddled with his red tie.

Bob went back to the outer office, and as he poured himself more coffee Susan Goodman, the part-time junior secretary, walked in. She was a very pretty woman of perhaps twenty-eight or thirty. Bob introduced himself and introduced Perez and Bobbitt.

Seating herself, Goodman said she doubted she could shed much light on what happened to "poor Mr. Berkman."

Perez asked her the usual run of questions.

"Do you happen to know who he met for lunch?"

"No, but I think it was at the La Jolla Country Club."

"Oh?" The detectives were suddenly quite interested.

"How do you know that?"

"Well, he said something in passing about the food there." She smiled self-consciously. "I'm getting married soon, and my family's thinking of having the reception there. He said the food was excellent."

"When did he tell you this?"

"At one point that afternoon he called me into his office to go over some calls he wanted me to make. To suppliers."

Perez was busy scribbling notes.

Bob asked if she had been in the outer office during Berkman's meeting with James Cunningham.

Goodman looked down. "Yes, I was here."

"Can you tell us anything about the meeting or their relationship?"

Goodman clenched her hands together and hesitated. "Well, I don't know what they discussed, but I know voices were raised. Quite a bit. That was true of their last few meetings, but this time, it seemed to grow quite heated."

Perez changed his expression, and asked, "Could you hear what they were saying?"

"No. Only that they were arguing."

Bobbitt spoke up. "How long was the meeting, and how soon did the arguing start?"

"The meeting lasted about half an hour. I'd say voices were raised after the first ten minutes or so."

"What did Mr. Berkman do after the meeting?"

"He got a file from that file cabinet, and then he made some phone calls."

Perez asked if she could direct them to any documents about Cunningham's investments.

"I'm afraid I've been instructed not to show you documents without a search warrant."

Perez looked annoyed. "All right. And who issued those instructions?"

"The mayor's chief of staff. Sandy Nelson."

"And when did you receive those instructions?"

"Early this morning."

Perez and Bob looked at each other.

Perez asked a few more routine questions, and then thanked her for her time. Since she made no sign of leaving the office, the three men got up to take their leave. Goodman struggled to smile as she said good-bye.

11

In the elevator, Perez said "okay kid, good questions. We'll alert the chief about what just happened. In the meantime we'll get a search warrant."

"And," Bob said, "we need to talk to Florence Russo again."

"Yeah, we do. Definitely. And we need to talk to the staff at that country club."

"The Cunninghams." Bobbitt smirked. "Just what we need. The press will go nuts."

Perez stared at him and clenched his jaw.

In the parking lot Bob asked, "You know anything about this particular Cunningham?"

"Not really. I'm pretty sure he's one of the younger ones."

"Is the Cunningham fortune intact?"

"Couldn't say. We'll need to find out."

Bob drove back downtown and found Cathy. She said Duane was tied up but should be free in an hour. Bob spent the hour in the DA's library, where the elderly and kind archivist helped him look things up in old newspaper files.

The world was still a year away from computer-based search engines.

The rows of file cabinets containing newspaper stories reminded Bob of the summer he spent as a college intern at the *Washington Post*. They didn't know what to do with him most days, so they had him work in what was called the morgue, filing away clippings. He was bored out of his mind. He was living in an attic sublet without air conditioning and had never been more miserable.

He found a thick file of clippings about the Cunningham family and also consulted *Who's Who*. James—one of "the" Cunninghams—was twenty-eight and divorced. He had gone to Stanford, dropped out after his first year for reasons that were not specified, and finished his bachelor's degree at San Francisco State. A picture of him in a tuxedo at a charity event showed a patrician young man with a studied smile. He was standing next to a woman in a stunning gown, identified in the article as the family's "matriarch," Maude Strauss Cunningham. She looked like a very well-preserved sixty-year-old.

There was nothing in the archives about Gerald Otley, but Philip, the archivist, said he'd call a friend at *The New York Times*. Bob thanked him and headed to Duane's office.

"So? Anything?" Duane asked as soon as Bob walked through the door.

Bob poured himself coffee and recounted the meeting. Cathy joined them just as he began.

Duane looked stunned. "James Cunningham. Jesus."

"We'll have to speak to him," Bob said, with trepidation.

"Yes," Duane replied. "Of course. But we'll have to think carefully about when and how."

Bob thought that was a bit odd. Surely he was now a suspect. But he said nothing.

Duane pulled himself out of a fog. "Cathy, tell the forensic guy to look for references to Cunningham and report back ASAP."

Just then another secretary stuck her head in the office to say that Chief Murphy was on the phone.

Duane picked up and listened. "Right. Three-thirty, here," and then hung up.

"There'll be a strategy meeting this afternoon with the cops. In an hour or so they'll have a warrant for the rest of Berkman's office files. Bob, a clerk will meet the detectives and deliver the files to the accountant. In the meantime meet with him, see what's what."

Bob felt awkward but said what had been weighing on him since he arrived. "Right. Will do. I hate to mention," here he stopped and cleared his throat, "I need some time to prepare for the bar exam. I keep hearing how tough it is here. High flunk rate."

"Yes, of course. We'll get someone in to help you, there are bar coaches available. We'll carve out some time for that, I promise."

12

Cathy took Bob to a tiny, windowless office and introduced him to Jeff Adelman, the forensic accountant. He smiled without getting up and they shook hands. A man of about fifty in a rumpled polyester suit, he looked like he hadn't had a good night's sleep in months. Three empty coffee cups sat in front of him on the desk.

"I'll leave you to it," Cathy said.

Adelman was surrounded by open files, a computer, a calculator, and several volumes of the California Commercial Code. Bob filled him in on what he had heard that morning.

"Obviously," Bob continued, "Mr. Cunningham is now a suspect. We need to know what he and Berkman argued about. Are there any clues here?"

"Maybe. I need additional files"—Bob told him they were coming—"but it looks like Cunningham was heavily invested in building projects that did not do well financially."

"So he lost money?"

"Could have. Some of Berkman's recent projects seem not to have done well. Houses didn't sell, prices had to be lowered, that kind of thing. Some projects lost money, some just about broke even. Berkman would often go back to investors to ask for more capital. My guess is, he over-promised them. And he may have had trouble paying back some loans."

"Where did he find his investors?"

"Most were common sources—banks, real estate holding companies. And then some private investors, like Cunningham. It looks to me like maybe he went to individuals when he reached his limit with more traditional sources. A bank or a holding company will only invest so much. Also, some of Berkman's cost estimates were off."

Bob thought for a moment. "And what about Lincoln Savings?"

"That's where things get interesting. Lincoln was heavily invested, often in stages."

"And they got a share of the equity in return?"

"Yes. At one point, Berkman had to offer them more than the usual return. Looks like he needed more capital for this project in Oceanside."

Adelman explained that Berkman would usually set aside some units as rentals but retain ownership. Over time, the units appreciated, and he built up substantial equity. Then he'd sell them at a profit. Lincoln got a piece of that.

"Is that legal?"

"So far I'd say yes, perfectly legal."

Bob was taking notes. "And is there any relationship between Cunningham and Lincoln?"

"I need more information. But my guess—and it's just a guess at this point—is that Berkman redirected some of Cunningham's money intended for a project in Chula Vista to a project in Oceanside, where Lincoln was also invested."

"Chula Vista is where?"

"South of downtown. Oceanside is way up in North County."

"So Cunningham might have found out, and been upset?"

"I'd say that's a possibility. But don't take that to the bank just yet."

"Is moving money from one project to another like that legal?"

"It depends on the terms of their contract, which I don't have yet."

Bob wrote CONTRACT in capital letters in his notes. "Anything else look legally fishy? Anything to suggest a motive for murder?"

"Berkman was sometimes tardy in paying his contractors. But not by a lot, and not enough to get him killed, as far as I can see. So far. And I haven't uncovered any illegality. Yet. As for murder," Adelman paused and sipped his coffee, "that's your department, not mine."

Bob smiled. "This is really helpful. Thanks. The rest of the files should be here soon, we needed a warrant."

13

Bob went back to his office and looked at his watch; it was already 2:15, and he realized he hadn't had lunch. He went to Cathy's office and she read his mind.

"There's a tuna sandwich waiting for you in the library."

He smiled and thanked her, then wolfed down the sandwich and started typing up his notes on his new Macintosh. He accidentally erased things as he was typing— he missed typewriters—and had to start over. He stopped once to call Marcus but got no answer. He reminded himself to hook up their answering machine. Marcus was hopeless with electronic devices. In Cambridge Bob had once come home to find the VCR disassembled after Marcus had tried to get it to work.

After a while Cathy stuck her head in and told him it was time for the meeting with the cops. They all crowded into the DA's office and sat around the conference table.

Stevens spoke first. "Okay, where are we?"

Duane and Perez gave summaries of what they knew so far. At the mention of Cunningham's name, Bob thought Stevens seemed suddenly more engaged, though he considered the DA hard to read. He remembered his father once telling him that being hard to read was an essential skill for a good lawyer.

Duane asked Bob for a recap of his meeting with the accountant; Bob told the story as straightforwardly as he could. He mostly looked at his notes as he spoke, but whenever he looked up, he got the distinct impression he was telling Duane things he didn't want to hear. Stevens, on the other hand, was interested. The cops looked intrigued, especially Perez.

"Okay," Chief Murphy said. "So clearly we need to go back to this Russo woman. She withheld information. Why? And we need to interview Cunningham and get his fingerprints. There were prints on two glasses in the office— one broken, on the floor, and one on the side table—and we don't yet know who they belong to. And we need to find out about that lunch at the country club."

"What about the warrant? Do we have the rest of Berkman's files?" Duane asked.

"On their way," Perez replied.

"Good," said Duane. "Maybe we should wait and let the accountant go through them before we talk to Cunningham. He'll lawyer up immediately—and if the press gets wind of his involvement, they'll go berserk."

Stevens put down his pen; he had been jotting notes. His left hand opened and closed as usual. "I want Russo interrogated tomorrow. Bring her to the station, do it there. Rattle her. That okay, Chief?"

Murphy nodded.

"Let's see if she tells us anything about Cunningham, or if the accountants do after they have those files. I've told Adelman to bring in help to go through everything as quickly as possible. In the meantime, set up a first meeting with Cunningham. He lives in LA but he has a beach house in Carlsbad. It's summer, he may be there."

Carlsbad was one of the beach towns that stretched between the northern tip of San Diego and Camp Pendleton, the huge Marine base that separated greater San Diego from greater Los Angeles. It was a common opinion that without Pendleton the whole region would be one giant megalopolis. It was also common knowledge that a substantial portion of the young male marines at Pendleton frequented San Diego's gay bars.

Stevens went on. "If he wants to lawyer up, he can lawyer up. There's an eyewitness—or an ear-witness—to a big argument. That's a fact. He can't deny it. And it's beginning to look like he may have had motive. Get a warrant for all of his financial records. And we should locate his ex-wife, talk to her too."

He then looked directly at Duane. "I'm not gonna worry about the press."

Duane frowned. "The Cunningham meeting was at two o'clock on Friday, but the ME says Berkman was murdered after five. We know Berkman was alive at four o'clock when he sent the staff home."

Stevens looked irritated. "So maybe Cunningham came back. Or he made a call and had someone else go ahead with the actual murder. Or had someone waiting. A chauffeur. An aide. His gardener. Whatever. That family has enough money to hire any thug in the world."

Duane sat back in his chair.

"Right," Murphy said. "Let's get to it."

Stevens stood up. The meeting was over.

14

Bob made it home by 5:30. Marcus was almost finished painting the living room—and himself, Bob noticed. "Um," he said with a laugh, "I'm glad you managed to get some of that paint on the walls."

"Very funny." Marcus climbed down from the ladder and kissed Bob on the cheek, careful not to get paint on his suit. "I'll take a shower."

Their house was in the San Diego neighborhood called Normal Heights. The name derived from the long-gone state normal school for teachers, and they were tickled by the idea of living in a neighborhood labeled "normal."

Perched on a bluff, it was a neighborhood in transition. Only partly gentrified, some blocks were lovely and serene with well-kept lawns, while others looked a bit rough. The rougher areas had old apartment buildings and houses that looked neglected, with chain-link fences and beat-up pickup trucks in gravel driveways. There was a giant red neon sign proclaiming the neighborhood's name across Adams Avenue, the main thoroughfare, which separated the north and south sections and held the usual urban mix of antique stores, an old diner, and a second-hand book shop. Everyone said it was a neighborhood on the way up, but they were advised to confine their search to the section north of Adams.

One of the first things they noticed was that everyone in San Diego seemed obsessed with real estate and talked about it constantly, including the price of houses.

The house they'd chosen was a short drive from Hillcrest, the center of the gay community, and convenient to several major freeways, making it an easy commute to work for both of them. It was a comfortable ranch in the ubiquitous style known as California Mission—white stucco, red tile roof. It had been built in the 1920s, just before the Wall Street crash, and had been updated and well cared for; the professional inspection revealed no major problems. With its beautiful wood floors, three large bedrooms and two bathrooms, a working fireplace and lots of original dark wood, Bob could see that Marcus loved it the moment they walked in.

"Of course, in a big quake, it's curtains for a house this old," the inspector said cheerily as Bob and Marcus stared at him. "But that's true of ninety percent of the houses in this part of town. And you're not that close to the major fault line."

They'd both swallowed hard and plunked down their deposit.

That night they went to California Cuisine, a restaurant in Hillcrest on the main drag, University Avenue. It was on a busy block that held a gay bar, a new gay bookstore called Obelisk, and a crowded coffee bar called Soho. They were seated outdoors, on the large patio. It was another perfect evening weather-wise.

Bob looked around at the other patrons, mostly gay male couples and groups.

"Is every white guy in California twenty-five and blond?"

"Yes," Marcus replied as he looked at the menu. "It's a state law. No one older than thirty is allowed to come in. The university had to get a special bill passed in the state legislature to hire me. You might be deported because of your black hair."

Bob threw his head back and laughed.

"So, catch the killer yet?" Marcus asked after they gave their order to the waiter—impossibly gorgeous, Bob thought, and, of course, impossibly blond.

"Well, there's a suspect. James Cunningham."

Marcus's glass of water stopped halfway to his mouth.

"One of 'the' Cunninghams?"

Bob nodded.

"My God. They own half of Los Angeles. Maybe more."

"I know."

"This could turn into the murder trial of the decade. If he did it."

"I know. Great way to begin, huh?"

"Did he do it??"

"Who knows." Bob laughed. "So far it's just some pieces that might suggest motive. Circumstantial."

"Be careful, pooh. Can you imagine the lawyers he could hire?"

Bob sighed. "Probably a whole army of them. Wearing great suits. I could pick up some style tips. That could be useful. I need a West Coast wardrobe. We both do."

Marcus looked worried. "This is the kind of case that makes or breaks lawyers."

Bob tried to smile. "Well luckily I wouldn't be the actual prosecutor. If it comes to that. Maybe he didn't do it."

Bob changed the subject. "Did you make it up to campus?"

"I did. No one was around except the staff, who are all very nice. They had two students there to help me unpack my books. Both of them could be male models."

"Oh?" Bob smiled. "Just remember what I told you when you proposed."

Marcus laughed. "I remember. "If I cheat on you you'll

remove part of my anatomy."

"And now I have friends in the DA's office. They'll never charge me."

Marcus guffawed.

15

On the way to wash up after dinner Marcus saw a colleague from UCSD, Jim Stewart, at an indoor table. Jim waved him over, greeted Marcus warmly, and introduced his wife, Arlene. They, too, had just finished eating and suggested Marcus and Bob join them for coffee.

"And the chocolate tart, it's to die for," added Arlene.

It occurred to Marcus that Stewart, a San Diego native who followed local politics closely, might offer some insights into the situation facing Bob.

"Jim," he said, "Bob just started as an Assistant DA . . . and he's been assigned to the Berkman murder!"

His voice expressed pride, along with an undercurrent of hesitation. Like Bob, Marcus wasn't sure they should be talking about the case.

Jim whistled. "Wow. Quite a way to begin."

"You're telling me," Bob replied with an ironic grin as both the Stewarts laughed.

Marcus went on. "Do you know much about the Berkmans? Anything that might be helpful?"

"Well," Jim paused. "I've met them both, several times, and served on a city committee that Amy chaired."

Bob perked up. The dessert helped, and it was good coffee. "What can you tell me about her?"

"She's a smooth operator. Emphasis on operator."

Bob was intrigued. "How do you mean?"

"Of course she has her eye on higher office, everyone pretty much knows that, has from the very beginning. I wouldn't be surprised if she jumps into the Senate race in '92. I've watched her rise over the years, since she was on the city council."

"And?"

"Well, there's something very calculated about her. Of course that's true of almost all politicians, but it's pronounced in her. You get the sense, or at least I have, that she doesn't have core beliefs, or any real beliefs at all. She sniffs the wind. And she's good at it."

Bob silently digested this new, somewhat cynical, opinion.

"She reminds me of Reagan, actually," Arlene said. "Too smooth. Always checking her camera angles. Nice rhetoric but bad policies."

Bob was now glad they'd run into the Stewarts. He wanted to hear more.

"And what about Sam? What about the marriage?"

"Sam is—was—all about money," Jim said. Arlene nodded agreement. "I don't think he cared much about politics at all. You got the sense . . ." Jim hesitated.

"Of?" Bob asked.

Arlene replied. "I'll say it. Jim can be too nice. You got the sense that maybe this was a marriage of convenience. An arrangement more than a love story."

Bob leaned forward. "How so?"

"Amy needed money. She was from a pretty modest background. And Sam needed . . ."

"Political legitimacy?" Marcus offered.

"Yes. And political connections. They remind me a little

of another political couple I've been keeping an eye on, the Clintons of Arkansas."

Neither Marcus nor Bob had heard of them.

"The Clintons?" Marcus asked.

"Yeah. Word is he may be the Democratic presidential nominee sooner or later. He's governor of Arkansas. Everyone in Arkansas knows he's a philanderer, but so far it hasn't hurt him politically. She's a very smart and ambitious lawyer. They met at Yale Law. They have a young daughter."

"Did Sam have enemies?" Bob asked. He remembered a favorite saying of his mother's: "in for a penny, in for a pound." Might as well get as much information as he could.

"Oh, I don't think you get that rich in Southern California without enemies. Huge fortunes are made here in property development. The population is always growing." He paused. "And there's a general sense around town that Sam plays it all a bit fast and loose. Nothing illegal, probably, but who knows?"

Bob was lost in thought. They finished dessert, paid their respective bills, and said good night out on the sidewalk. Jim wished Bob luck with the case. He thanked them for their insight.

In the car on the way home, Bob remarked, "You know, Jim and Arlene reminded me a bit of—"

Marcus finished the sentence. "George Burns and Gracie Allen."

"Yes!"

"Yeah, Marcus said. "I thought of that the first time I met them, at one of the dinners when I was being recruited."

"Funny."

"You'll have to meet Curt McCubbins, another colleague. He's the spitting image of Michael Landon."

"Who's Michael Landon?"

Marcus stared in disbelief. "Oh my God. You really are young, aren't you? Michael Landon, one of the brothers on *Bonanza*."

Bob shrugged; he had no idea what *Bonanza* was.

"What do you think? About that they said." Marcus asked.

"Intriguing, I'll say that much."

"Well, good. Now forget about the case. I'm going to have my way with you when we get home. After all, I bought you dinner."

"Why Captain Butler, how you talk."

When they got home, the phone was ringing. Cathy told Bob the police were going to interview Florence Russo at 10:00 the next morning at the central police station; he was to meet Duane at the office at 9:30 and they'd go over together.

Bob sighed as he hung up the phone.

16

Bob met Duane as instructed, and Duane drove them to police headquarters, a modern, nondescript building not far from their office.

"The boss is pushing hard on Cunningham," Duane said. "He even wants a search of his properties for the murder weapon. But that kind of knife is so common, probably nine out of ten households have one. And Cunningham is smart enough to clean it off or get rid of it. So far I've convinced him to forget the search, but he keeps bringing it up."

Bob was surprised. "Raised voices behind a closed door

doesn't mean murder."

Duane laughed. "Did they teach you that at Harvard? By the way, Cathy tracked down Cunningham's ex. Her name is Judith Powers. She lives in LA but she's out of town and her maid says she doesn't know where, or when she'll be back."

Bob hesitated for a moment, but decided to go ahead and ask.

"Why is Fred so keen as Cunningham as the murderer?"

Duane sighed. "I don't know. Maybe because he's the only suspect at the moment. Maybe it's all the publicity, the pressure."

"Could it be," Bob said before he realized what he was saying, "that convicting a Cunningham of murder would be a real coup for his career?"

Duane looked uncomfortable. "He doesn't really operate that way."

Bob shifted in his seat but said no more. He had clearly hit a nerve.

They met Perez and Bobbitt in the detective's squad room on the third floor and followed them to an area outside the interview room. Duane and Bob were to watch and listen to the questioning of Florence Russo through the two-way mirror. Then, if additional pressure was needed, it would be Duane who would join them.

The space was small and hot, and Bob began to sweat. The mirrored window was dirty, and there was a speaker in the wall that could be turned on or off on either side.

At exactly 10:00 a.m., Russo entered the interview room through a door opposite the mirror. She was with her attorney, whom she introduced as Lucy Hargrove. Hargrove looked vaguely familiar to Bob, but he couldn't place her.

She was perhaps in her mid-thirties, beautiful and blond, perfectly poised. Russo's face, on the other hand, looked hardened into a slight smile, and she looked older than she had just twenty-four hours before.

Duane spoke under his breath. "So she's lawyered up. Not good."

"Do you know the attorney?"

"Oh yeah. She's good. Very good. Judges love her."

Bob stared at her. She reminded him of Eva Marie Saint in *North By Northwest* with her blond, icy demeanor, but there was something else about her that looked familiar. He couldn't put his finger on it.

Bob noticed that a camera had been set up and was recording the meeting, and Bobbitt switched it on. That was unusual at this stage of an investigation, Bob knew.

Perez began the questioning.

"Miss Russo, yesterday you told us briefly about the meeting Mr. Berkman held with Mr. Cunningham on Friday afternoon. Is there anything you'd like to add to your description of that meeting? Before you answer, I should point out that withholding evidence from the police in a murder investigation is a serious matter, and can lead to criminal charges."

Hargrove spoke up immediately. "There's no need to get tough, Detective. My client met with you yesterday voluntarily. She has nothing to hide."

Russo looked down at her lap. "I know you spoke to Susan, and she told you more about the meeting than I did." She looked up. "I did not intend to withhold anything. I'm sorry if you formed that impression."

"Go on."

"Mr. Berkman has a bit of a temper. Had, I should say."

She paused. "We all do, I guess. His didn't come out very often, but sometimes it did. Hearing him raise his voice, either on the phone or in a meeting, was not all that unusual, at least to me. I just did not think it was important. I've been with him longer than Susan, seen and heard more."

Bob noticed she pronounced the t in "often."

"You'll have to do better than that, Miss Russo. What was the nature of the disagreement between Mr. Berkman and Mr. Cunningham? You must see Mr. Berkman's paperwork. We assume you keep his files. I think you know more than you're saying."

Both Perez and Bobbitt stared at her intently and did not break their gaze.

Russo swallowed hard and took a sip from the small bottle of Perrier she had produced from her purse.

"Mr. Cunningham was rather heavily invested in some of our building projects. I don't think he felt his money was being used well, and was, I would guess, worried about his investment."

"What project specifically? And how 'heavily' is 'heavily'?"

"As far as I'm aware, Mr. Cunningham invested $10 million in a project to build houses and condominiums on a parcel of land in Chula Vista."

"What was the total budget for that project?"

"Initial estimates were around $60 million."

"Had the two of them argued before? About this or anything else?"

"Not as far as I am aware."

"What was the source of Cunningham's unhappiness?"

Bob noticed that Perez had not once moved, or taken his gaze off of Russo. He knew what he was doing.

"I don't recall all the details. But the project in Chula

Vista was very similar to a project in Oceanside. Mr. Berkman thought of them as one big enterprise—they were being built at the same time, and the housing units were similar. Costs were mounting rather rapidly at both locations, but especially in Oceanside, largely due to some unexpected geological issues. The pre-sale of units was lagging."

"And?"

Russo hesitated and glanced at her attorney, who nodded slightly. "And Mr. Berkman may have redirected some of the money from one site to the other. As I said, they were quite similar in his mind. And I don't have any idea what Mr. Berkman did or did not tell Mr. Cunningham when they initially discussed his investment."

Perez let that sink in, then continued.

"Did you see the contract itself?"

"I placed it in the file at one point, but I did not read it."

"Do you know if Mr. Cunningham was offered any particular return on his investment?"

"I do not. I told you I didn't read the contract."

Perez continued to stare at her, until she added, obviously uncomfortably, "I do know that in the past Mr. Berkman has offered returns to individual investors in the realm of seven to eight percent."

"Over what period of time?"

"A year, give or take."

Outside the interview room Duane whistled and glanced at Bob. "That's high for the first year. Even out here."

"Is there anyone else with whom Mr. Berkman argued recently, as far as you are aware?"

"Not to my knowledge."

"What was Mr. Cunningham's demeanor when he left the meeting?"

"Normal. Composed."

"So he didn't storm out?"

"No."

"And Mr. Berkman's demeanor?"

"I don't know. He closed the door to the inner office and made some phone calls."

"Do you know to whom those calls were made?"

"I do not."

"So you don't keep a log of his calls?"

"No. He never asked for that."

After a few more perfunctory questions, Perez said, "All right, Miss Russo. Thank you for the information. Please be aware that if you have withheld any vital information, the consequences could be serious. Here's my card if you think of anything else." Perez emphasized the word "withheld."

Hargrove spoke. "She's told you everything she knows, as advised."

"I certainly hope so. Thank you for coming in."

Hargrove glanced at the two-way mirror as she was leaving and nodded.

17

The post-mortem on the interview was done in Chief Murphy's office.

"Okay," Murphy says. "So Cunningham was not getting a good return. And Berkman may have moved money around. But is that enough for murder when you're from one of the two or three richest families in the state?" Murphy sounded and looked skeptical.

Duane spoke up as he took off his glasses. "We have to find out how much this particular Cunningham has. I've got accountants looking at that right now."

Murphy nodded.

"But of course," Duane went on, "$10 million ain't chicken feed, even if you're rich. And no one likes to be played. Maybe he thought he had been played."

Murphy nodded reluctantly. "Okay. Next step, interview with Cunningham. Do we know where he is?"

Bobbitt responded as he straightened his red tie. "He's at his house in Carlsbad. Apparently he goes back and forth between there and his house in Bel Air, which is next door to the Reagans' new place." It was also, Bob knew, considered the toniest part of Los Angeles.

Bobbitt smirked. "The day he met with Berkman he was staying at the beach house in Carlsbad. He stayed there Friday and Saturday night and went back to LA on Sunday."

"The day the murder hit the papers," Perez added, sounding like he was thinking out loud.

Bobbitt nodded. "He stayed in Bel Air Sunday night, then came back down to the beach late the next day."

"And how do we know all this?" Murphy asked.

"His Los Angeles butler." Bobbitt smirked.

"So he knows we're interested in talking to him, or at least in his whereabouts. We should get to him right away," Murphy said. "Before he has too much time to concoct a story. If he needs a story. Offer to bring him in at night."

Perez frowned and was about to speak.

Murphy cut him off. "I know. Not the usual thing. But we don't want it all over the news. We could end up with a real shitstorm."

Perez was clearly not happy but said nothing further.

On the drive back to their office Duane said, "So. Did you believe Miss Russo?"

Bob wasn't sure, and said so. "I mean, she may have been trying to protect her boss, that would be natural. Or maybe she really has overheard arguments before and didn't think it was a big deal. And of course, she had no way of knowing he'd end up dead that night."

Duane was pensive as they walked into their building. "I'll report to the boss. You check in with the accountants."

In the hallway Cathy handed Bob a slip of paper with a name and a phone number. He looked at her, perplexed.

"Your bar coach. She'll drop some stuff off this morning."

Philip, the archivist, caught him in the hallway. Something about the man reminded Bob of an older Cary Grant, with his distinguished appearance and graying hair..

"I heard back from my friend in New York," Philip said. "I've got some information about Otley." He led Bob into the archive office and shut the door.

"My friend at the *Times* checked their files and also checked with their local crime reporter, who now works in Miami. Otley is a former male model who was once arrested for soliciting in Manhattan. When he was quite young."

Bob let that sink in.

Philip went on. "He apparently had an arrest for working as a male prostitute, but he took a deal, pleaded guilty to a misdemeanor, and later charges were dropped, although it's unclear how or why. He now works for an art gallery."

Bob asked the obvious question. "Did he solicit men or women?"

"Apparently, both. The arrest was for soliciting a well-known society matron."

Philip handed Bob his notes and a copy of a photo that

had been faxed. The photo was grainy but Otley appeared to be a well-dressed man in his thirties, standing with a group of typically chic New Yorkers at a gallery opening, all holding cocktails and looking successful and prosperous— and completely self-satisfied.

Bob stared at the photo for a long moment.

"Thanks so much, Philip. This is helpful. Very confusing, but helpful."

18

Bob went down to the front of the building for some fresh air. His friend the guard waved as he stepped outside and took a deep breath. He could smell and feel the ocean in the air. He closed his eyes and wondered what Marcus was doing.

Maybe we should have just moved here even if I didn't have a job. I'd have found something, he told himself. He had the same feeling in his stomach he had when he was a little boy and his mother took him to the train station to say good-bye to a visiting aunt. When the two adults talked, Bob wandered a bit, and got too close to the track. When the train approached the station, he froze, until his mother's steady hand pulled him back. In a strange way, this case felt the same way: he was getting too close to the track.

He walked back inside.

Jeff Adelman and his assistants had been moved to a larger office, this one with a window. They were seated around a table laden with files, law books, documents, and two computers. Cookie and doughnut crumbs were everywhere. Adelman introduced his two colleagues as Richard and Oliver. They smiled and nodded. Both looked like younger versions of Adelman, and like him they wore inexpensive polyester suits.

Must be a thing, Bob thought. Accountants and policemen and polyester.

Aloud, he asked, "So, what have you found?"

"So far, nothing illegal," Adelman said, sipping coffee and spilling a few drops on the papers in front of him. "Berkman seems to have been an expert at moving funds around, getting private investors to fill in gaps in funding, that sort of thing, but nothing not kosher. At least not yet." Oliver and Richard both nodded.

"Do you have a copy of the contract between Berkman and James Cunningham?"

"Yes, perfectly standard."

"It's for a project in Chula Vista?"

"It doesn't name a location, it refers only to 'the development of new homes and condominium communities in San Diego county.' It looks like Cunningham's money was first used in Chula Vista, and then some was shifted to Oceanside. The Oceanside project turned into a nightmare, cost overruns all over the place."

Bob was busy taking notes. "I see. That tracks with what we just heard from one of Berkman's employees. Was Cunningham in danger of losing his money? Or getting little return on his investment?"

"Hard to say. I'd say the jury would have still been out on that when Berkman died. So to speak." Adelman drank more coffee.

"Do we know Cunningham's net worth yet? How significant was this investment to him?"

"I'm told we'll have access to his records later today."

"Okay, thanks. All very helpful."

On his way back to his office, Cathy stopped Bob in the hallway. "We've arranged for you to have lunch with some of the other ADAs. In the large conference room. And your bar coach is dropping some stuff off in your office."

The "stuff" was a huge pile of loose-leaf notebooks. A genial young woman greeted him as Bob walked in. "Hi! I'm Jennifer. I decided to drop these off." She was casually dressed in linen slacks and looked to be about 35. She wore her blond hair in a pageboy and was very tan.

Bob shook her hand and introduced himself. He stared at the notebooks. "Thanks. I think."

Jennifer laughed. "Don't worry. Most of this is stuff you already know. Some of it is California-specific. That's where I can be the most help to you."

"Great," Bob said, "although the sight of the notebooks made him a bit queasy.

"So you were an editor of the *Harvard Law Review*. Impressive."

"Thanks."

"I went to UCLA, undergrad and law. Then I was a public defender for a while out in Bakersfield, but couldn't stand the heat out there."

"I can imagine." Bakersfield, about 100 miles north and east of LA, far from the ocean, was unpleasantly hot and dry. After an instant Bob realized by "heat" Jennifer could have meant either working as a public defender or the literal climate, or both.

"And I realized I'm a born teacher. And I like to set my own hours. So I do this instead."

They discussed how often they should meet, how to

organize Bob's preparation, when he should plan to take the bar, and a few other details. Cathy then stuck her head in and said lunch would start soon.

"You've got my number," Jennifer said. "Call me when you're ready for the first meeting. I can work around your schedule."

A few minutes later Cathy walked Bob to the conference room where Duane and several other ADAs were waiting. Duane made the introductions and apologized that not everyone could be there.

Bob's peers, three men and four very attractive women, were all smiles and welcomes. Over sandwiches, they exchanged pleasantries, asking Bob about Marcus, about their house, how they were settling in, and gave out tips about studying for the bar exam.

"Jennifer is great," the friendliest of the group said. "She'll get you through it."

Bob imprinted his name: Billy Louis. Nice guy. Outgoing.

After the sandwiches came coffee and cookies. The talk turned to the Berkman murder, and Bob detected some jealousy that he had gotten to work on such an important case right off the bat. Of course they all understood that he got the assignment in large part because he had not yet passed the bar, and thus could not be the attorney of record on any other case, or appear in court on behalf of the DA. But still, everyone knew, this was the kind of case that didn't come along very often.

The tone was friendly, but the talk about the case reminded Bob a little of his conversations with some of the people he'd known in law school. Everyone was polite, civil, good-natured, but a raging competitiveness lurked just underneath the surface. He remembered a conversation with his father, who had also gone to an Ivy League law school. "You won't find a lot of true friends there. Watch your back."

19

When lunch broke up Bob asked to see Duane. He soon filled him in on what he had learned, both from the accountants and about Otley.

The Otley news left Duane thunderstruck. He got up and paced up and down.

"Of course," Bob offered, "the bequest could have nothing unseemly about it. It could have nothing to do with Otley's former life."

"But then what's the connection? It's clearly suspicious."

Bob nodded.

"If it was an illicit relationship of some kind," Duane said as he sat down at his desk again, "why not pay cash? Why make it public in a will?" He drummed his fingers on his desk.

Bob couldn't think of a reason and said nothing, and they sat in silence for a few moments.

"Well, we'll have to get to the bottom of it," Duane finally said. "We'll need to ask the mayor if she knows him, or knows his name. And we'll need to interview Otley. Maybe before we speak to the mayor. Or after. I need to think about that. You may have to fly to New York. But first we need to concentrate on Cunningham. The boss wants the full-court press on him."

All of this was sinking in for both of them when Cathy

stuck her head in. "The green eyeshade man needs to see Bob."

Bob found him waiting for him in his office.

"We have the info on Cunningham's finances. He has a net worth of roughly $95 million, mostly invested in the usual places, blue chip stocks, bonds. In addition, receives a monthly allowance from a family trust of $10,000."

"And the investment with Berkman?"

"Came out of his portfolio. My guess—and it's a fair assumption at this point—is that he invested with Berkman in the hopes of getting a higher return and beefing up his earnings. He might have been planning to spend what he earned from the deal, or he might have been planning to add the profit to his capital. No way to know based on the numbers."

"I see."

"Again, it's a guess, but I'd say that people with net worth in that neighborhood are often looking for ways to beef up their capital. Overall the portfolio has been earning three percent, which isn't very good these days, but of course, the higher the return, the higher the risk. Cunningham may have thought a real estate investment with Berkman was a good bet. The Cunningham family first got rich over land. Maybe it's in the blood."

Bob nodded. "Anything else?"

"His expenses were high. The house in Bel Air, the beach house, staff. Custom-made suits. He did not live modestly."

"Okay, thanks."

Bob went back to Duane to report what he had just heard. Duane was on the phone. He was saying "I'll have to check with Fred and get back to you."

"That was Chief Murphy. Cunningham's attorney called. They know we want to speak to them, and they want a meeting to discuss how the interview will be conducted. It's tentatively scheduled for tomorrow morning."

"Is that kind of meeting usual?"

"It's not usual, but it's happened before. I need to clear it with Fred."

"I need to fill you in on what I just heard about Cunningham's finances."

Duane got up. "Walk with me."

As they walked toward the DA's office, Bob told him what he had just learned.

"So the money he invested with Berkman was a good chunk of his cash. I mean, he'd still be filthy rich if he lost it, but it's not like he was worth a billion dollars."

"No."

"That's what happens with some of these old wealthy families," Duane went on. "The wealth gets divided and dwindles with each new generation. Our guy is third generation. And there were a lot of kids in earlier generations. And I'm sure he hangs around with the super-rich."

As they reached the DA's office, Bob turned around, assuming Duane would want to talk to Fred alone, but Duane told him to stay.

Stevens was standing at a cabinet in the outer office, looking for a file. "What's up?"

They all walked into the inner office and sat at the conference table. Duane told him about the call from Murphy.

The DA stood up and walked over to the window. He waited a moment before speaking.

"Go ahead with his lawyer. But make clear our condition for the meet with Cunningham himself is that the two of you be there, and that Cunningham offer his fingerprints. We can do it at his beach house. And it needs to happen ASAP.

We can always haul him in later, parade him in front of the cameras, if we need to."

Duane nodded.

"What else is happening?" Fred asked as he sat back down.

Duane turned to Bob with an expression that said, *Talk*.

Bob quickly narrated everything he had learned. Fred listened and took a few notes, and looked uncomfortable at the mention of Otley, but quickly recovered his composure.

"Good work. Someone has to talk to this guy."

"Right. And we'll ask Amy if the name means anything to her." Duane stood to go, and Bob followed him out the door. He was learning that Fred was a man of few words.

"So," Duane said, "meet me at nine tomorrow morning at Murphy's office for the meet with Cunningham's lawyer."

"Are you sure you want me there?"

"Oh yeah. The more bodies on our side the better."

Bob spent the rest of the day looking through the notebooks Jennifer had left, making a few notes, but his thoughts kept returning to the case. His gut said Cunningham was not likely to be the killer. Too obvious: they argued, then Berkman is dead. If he planned it, he'd do it later, and somewhere else. If he did it in a blind fury, it would have happened when they argued, not hours later.

And what good would killing Berkman do? Would it guarantee a better return on his money? Probably just the opposite; the legal tangle after the death could delay things for quite a while.

And what about Otley? Could Berkman have hired him to . . . do what? Participate in a three-way? Or could it have been drugs? It wouldn't be that surprising if a gigolo or "escort" was also selling drugs. Or using. But a drug dealer would ask for cash up front, not wait for a bequest.

On the drive home, Bob realized he was avoiding an obvious question: Was Sam Berkman gay or bisexual?

He suddenly felt completely exhausted.

"Good God, you look terrible" was Marcus's greeting when he walked into the house.

Bob shot him a look. "Fuck you very much."

"Sorry. Bad day?"

"Not bad exactly. Full. And confusing. I need a shower. Then we're ordering pizza and having sex."

Marcus smiled. "Whatever you say, Perry Mason."

"Don't laugh. I'll be meeting Perry Mason tomorrow morning at nine a.m."

After the pizza, which they ate naked in bed, Bob relaxed. They got dressed and drove down Adams Avenue to a small gelato parlor in Kensington, just to the east of Normal Heights. Kensington was a bit farther down the road toward complete gentrification. They grabbed a small table in front of the store just as people were leaving and watched the peaceful passing scene, parents out with their children, a few gay and lesbian couples, everyone in a good mood. People were licking their gelato, laughing, or peering into store windows. The sun was beginning to go down and the cool breeze felt like a hug.

After four years they had reached the point as a couple where they knew what the other was thinking, at least most of the time. Marcus spoke first.

"Hard to reconcile all this California Cool with your murder, isn't it?"

Bob smiled. He felt safe.

He realized not much later that that was an illusion, one of the last of his innocent youth.

20

In the morning Bob arrived at police headquarters a few minutes before 9:00 and made his way to Chief Murphy's office on the top floor. Duane, Perez, and Bobbitt were huddled in one corner, while Murphy and a distinguished-looking man chatted nearby. Everyone held a cup of coffee. Duane introduced Bob to Sidney Carter, Cunningham's attorney.

Carter was handsome and well-groomed, wearing a suit that must have cost thousands. His shoes looked untouched by human hands. He smiled a dazzling smile.

"We're all here, let's sit," Murphy announced.

Everyone arranged themselves around the conference table, and Carter spoke first. "My client understands that he was one of the last people to see Sam Berkman alive. He wishes to help in any way he can. He knew Sam well."

Bob noted that Carter's description of the relationship was rather tepid.

Duane responded. "We appreciate that. We need to speak directly to him."

"Of course. We have nothing to hide."

Perez spoke. "We'll also need his fingerprints."

"Oh? Mr. Cunningham freely admits to meeting with Mr. Berkman that afternoon."

Murphy responded. "We understand. We need his prints. We're willing to conduct the interview at Mr. Cunningham's beach house to avoid unwarranted press speculation."

Carter nodded. "We appreciate that."

"We can take fingerprints while there."

Perez asked, "Is your client in Carlsbad?"

"Actually he's in San Francisco at the moment, but will be back down in Carlsbad by this weekend."

"Then," Murphy said, "please notify us as soon as he returns, and make your client available."

"Of course. Will do. We are fine with as many of you as you like sitting in. No two-way mirrors necessary."

Murphy and Duane smiled at that. Perez looked irritated.

Carter glanced at his very expensive-looking watch. "Is there anything else? I'm afraid I have to get to Los Angeles."

"Yes," Bob heard himself saying. He hadn't intended to speak, and was surprised that he had, but continued. "We'd appreciate it if Mr. Cunningham could turn over to us any additional documents in his possession that involve his investments in Berkman properties. Perhaps his accountant or business manager can do this before the interview."

"We anticipated this," Carter replied. "We're putting together the documents now and should be able to deliver them to you this afternoon."

Perez glanced in Bob's direction, looking impressed.

The chief closed the folder in front of him. "I think that covers everything. Thank you for coming in." He showed Carter to the door, closed it behind him, and returned to the conference table.

"I don't like it, doing it at his house," Perez said. "For one thing, that means we can't record the interview. And it's his home turf. He'll be comfortable."

"I know," Murphy responded. "But with the rich and mighty always a little patience."

"Who said that?" Duane asked.

"A police chief."

21

Cathy told them that Fred wanted to see them right away. They went directly to the sanctum, where Duane filled him in on the meeting with Cunningham's attorney.

"Okay, good," Fred responded. "What else? Anything turning up?"

"Well," Duane hesitated, "we have to start looking to see if there are any other suspects. There's not a lot there to suggest Cunningham is the perp."

"Why not?" Fred was clearly not happy.

"Well, he's not a dumb guy, I assume, and it would have been a dumb move—argue in the afternoon within earshot of witnesses, then come back and murder him later. And what's the motive? The accountants are saying Cunningham may have been unhappy with what Berkman had done with his money, but it was too early to know if the investment was going to pay off. And he was worth much more than that investment."

Fred absorbed that silently.

Duane said, "I want to have the accountants continue looking at Sam's other business dealings. See if there's anything there."

"Right."

"And we need to talk to the mayor as soon as possible."

"Yes. Next week." Fred stopped scowling and softened his voice. "Be careful there. She just lost her husband. What do we know about Cunningham's personal life?"

"Not much. Divorced. Ex-wife is away, we'll talk to her when she gets back. Bob?"

"We know he left Stanford after a year. We don't know

why, though it could be a lot of things. Did he flunk out? Did something happen? Was he caught cheating?"

"Well, dig into it. Go up there if you need to. I want to know everything about this guy."

Fred stood up to indicate the meeting was over.

As they walked back to their offices, Duane asked Bob if he had any contacts at Stanford.

"No, not one."

"Neither do I. What about your . . . partner?" Duane knew that Marcus would be working at UCSD.

Bob thought the pause was telling; Duane clearly wasn't ready for "boyfriend," much less "lover" or "husband" or other euphemisms. In fact, he thought, the rest of the world was no better off. Even after four years together Bob was sometimes at a loss as to how to introduce Marcus. Still, this can't be right, Bob thought, involving the spouse of an ADA in an investigation.

He said hesitantly, "I suppose I can ask him."

"Please. Otherwise someone will need to fly up there."

Bob went back to his office and shut the door. He paced back and forth. He wanted to tell Duane it was wrong to ask him to involve Marcus in the investigation of a suspect. It was awkward. Inappropriate. If it ever came out in court, it could be embarrassing. Even damaging.

But then he thought: Maybe this is how things go in the real, messy world. He remembered a conversation with his father and brother about lawyering. His father warned him about becoming a criminal lawyer. "Sooner or later, you'll feel like your hands are dirty." His brother nodded, though neither of them practiced criminal law. But in law school, those were the courses that excited Bob the most, and he couldn't really see himself as an associate in some kind of corporate law firm, toiling away at the least interesting parts of cases the partners didn't want to touch. The profession had changed since his father had set up a small practice with just two lawyers; offices like that were pretty much a thing of the past. And he thought a government job would be deadly dull.

Well, this case was interesting, all right. But it was only his first week on the job and his hands already felt dirty.

He sighed and picked up the phone. Marcus picked up on the first ring.

"Do you know anyone at Stanford?"

"That's how you greet me? Not 'Hi honey, I miss you, what are you doing?'"

"Hi honeybuns, I miss you. Do you know anyone at Stanford?"

Marcus laughed and thought for a minute. "Yes, someone in the History department. Any maybe someone in English, if they're still there."

"Okay, good. Well enough to ask a favor?"

"It depends on the favor."

"If you feel comfortable. Ask them if they might be able to find out why James Cunningham dropped out after only a year at Stanford?"

"Um, okay." Marcus paused. "What do I get in return?"

"I promise not to make fun of your cooking for six months."

"Deal."

Bob went to tell Duane, who suggested Bob take the time before the Cunningham interview to study for the bar.

He felt unexpected relief; he had been getting nervous every time he stared at the thick binders on this desk. He called Jennifer and suggested lunch at 1:00. He spent the rest of the morning reading the binder on Wills, Trusts, and Estates, his least favorite subject in law school, almost nodding off several times.

They met at a health food restaurant in Hillcrest and were able to get a table outside under a large awning. Jennifer ordered a salad, Bob a noodle-mushroom casserole, which he wolfed down; he hadn't realized how hungry he was.

He asked Jennifer for tips on how to organize his preparation, and she had quite a bit to say. It sounded like a standard recitation, but all of it was sensible and Bob was grateful for the advice.

Over coffee, Jennifer asked Bob how he and Marcus were settling in. Bob didn't know how Jennifer knew about Marcus—perhaps Duane told her—but Jennifer let drop that she lived with a woman and they'd all have to get together.

"How are you finding San Diego?" Jennifer asked as Bob paid the bill.

"Well, it takes some getting used to. I'm from the East, went to school there. The sun here is so strong! And I can't get used to the palm trees."

Jennifer laughed. "Wait until fall. You'll be wondering when the leaves will start to change, and they won't. In fact the best weather is in October and November. Warm but not hot, and cooler nights. Cleaner air. It's heaven."

"If you say so."

22

Bob went back to his binders, finishing up with the first and starting on California Criminal Law. That, at least, he found absorbing, as he had in law school. Throughout his three years at Harvard, he'd been surprised at how little interest he had in courses on subjects like Contracts and Civil Procedure—but criminal law he found fascinating. Real people doing bad things to each other, human psychology and behavior—that, to him, was what the law was about. One of his professors scoffed at the idea of his doing criminal law, and told him he had a naïve view of the world, a world where it was possible to separate the innocent from the guilty. Bob just smiled.

Perez called around 3:00 p.m. He and Bobbitt had been to the La Jolla Country Club and knew the identity of Sam's lunch partner that day; it was Cecil Richardson, a regular there. They were setting up a meeting.

An hour later Marcus called. "Something, maybe, at Stanford. I talked to my colleague in History, who did remember the James Cunningham incident. There was an allegation of his 'inappropriate' behavior on a date with another student. The administration agreed to drop the investigation if Cunningham agreed to transfer to another school. He did. There was a controversy about that, people thought he got off too easy, but generations of Cunninghams have gone to Stanford and donated heaps of money. There's a Cunningham Hall on campus and a Cunningham pool."

"Interesting. How inappropriate was the alleged behavior?"

"My contact didn't know. Apparently no one did. He did say a group of faculty women went to the president to complain about a cover-up and special treatment for the rich, but the administration held firm. I have a call in to the other guy I know, I'll see if he has any more details, or if he knows anything."

"Thanks."

"You're welcome. And you're taking me out to dinner. I

tried to bake something and it exploded in the oven."

Bob laughed. "Oh, but you tried, pumpkin. That's the important thing."

He reported what he had heard to Duane, who thought it was important. "Maybe this tells us Cunningham isn't a paragon of upper-class manners."

Bob was skeptical, and said so—they didn't have any real facts. "I mean, it could have been offering a young woman alcohol. It could have been misreading signals on a date. We don't know if it was violent in any way."

"No. But asking a Cunningham to leave campus isn't something you do over a slight misunderstanding. I mean, it could have meant the loss of millions."

Bob admitted that could be true but was still uncomfortable. He was close enough to his college years to know that students, especially first-years, do all sorts of things they later regret, and that administrators sometimes overreact. A friend of his when he was a freshman at Brown, in fact, had been hauled before a disciplinary board for wearing clothes that were deemed too "revealing" at a party. She'd had on a tank top.

"I just got word," Duane said, "we meet with Cunningham on Saturday morning. More of his business records arrived, the accountants are going through them, and they're going through more of Berkman's files. We may know more tomorrow or Friday. Check in with them every now and then. And Murphy will let us know if their investigators find any dirt in Berkman's linen. In the meantime, you'll have some time for bar prep."

Bob wasn't sure how much "meantime" there would be, what with all the information coming in, and he wasn't thrilled with the idea of losing his Saturday. But he nodded.

"Oh, and we're set to meet with the mayor on Tuesday."

Back in his office, he was about twenty minutes into the California Criminal binder when Cathy summoned him to a meeting with Fred. Duane was already there.

Fred started speaking before Bob had a chance to sit down. "Murphy called. Sam Berkman was seeing a therapist. We have the name." Fred handed Duane a piece of paper with a name and an address.

Duane stared at it. "She won't speak to us. Doctor-patient confidentiality."

"Probably not," Fred said. "But she might give us a hint. Perez is speaking to her tomorrow afternoon at two. Meet him there."

"Wild goose chase," Duane muttered to himself as he and Bob left.

"Still, it's interesting information," Bob said. "Something was up with Sam."

Duane seemed unpersuaded. "Half the population of California is in therapy."

When Bob got home that evening Marcus was just hanging up the phone. "That was my other contact at Stanford. Same story. No details."

Bob exhaled. "Okay, thanks. I really didn't want to ask you to do this, but Duane insisted."

"I live to serve."

Bob laughed. He changed into shorts and they sat on the patio with iced tea. "Let's just get take-out," Marcus said. "There's a new Thai restaurant that's supposed to be fabulous. I picked up a menu this afternoon."

While Marcus went to pick up the food, Bob took a shower. When he got out, there was a message on the machine from Adelman, the accountant, asking Bob to call him at home.

He sighed. He was beginning to resent how much his job intruded into his life. Last Sunday, the crime scene and the autopsy. The coming weekend, an interview with a suspect.

Bob knew from growing up that lawyer work could involve long hours and weekends; there were times when he hardly ever saw his father. Once, when he was around ten, his father was working on a particularly complex case that resulted in a trial in federal court that went on for eight weeks. His father was hardly ever home, and never in time for dinner, but one night made it back just as Bob and his brother were helping their mother with the dishes.

"Hi guys. I'm your dad," he said, and everyone laughed.

So Bob knew what he was getting into, or thought he did. But it was one thing to know something and another to experience it, to feel the pressure and the tension and the exhaustion.

As a friend of his once said about realizing that you were gay, there was knowing, and then there was knowing.

23

After the Thai food—Marcus was right, the food was terrific—Bob called Adelman back.

"I found something in Berkman's files that I thought you should know about right away."

"Okay." Bob fumbled around for a pad and pen, knocking over a box of leftovers in the process.

"Berkman had started putting funds into a Swiss bank account."

Bob swallowed hard. "Are you sure?"

"Yes. We can't verify it, of course, the Swiss won't allow that, but I've seen this type of account number before. I'm 99.9 percent certain."

"Is it a lot of money?"

"Millions."

Bob closed his eyes. "Okay, thanks. I think. We can go into it more in the morning."

"Copy that."

Bob cleaned up the spilled leftovers and then went back to the patio, where Marcus was wiping off the table.

"Are you okay? You look dazed."

"The plot just thickened."

"Can you tell me?"

Bob hesitated. "I probably shouldn't."

"Um, okay. Maybe we should watch a movie?"

"A comedy, please."

Marcus slipped *Some Like It Hot* into the VCR, and they settled on the couch. Some of the film, Bob had once told Marcus, had been filmed in San Diego, at the Hotel del Coronado. It was one of Bob's favorite movies, but he was so tired, he hardly noticed what was happening on the screen, even when Marilyn Monroe was singing in a scene he always had loved. At one point Marcus took his hand.

"It'll be okay."

Bob smiled. "From your mouth to God's ears." It was another one of his mother's expressions.

Marcus had heard her use the phrase; he smiled. "I love your mother. And not just because she taught you to cook."

Bob put his head in Marcus's lap, and Marcus rested a hand on his shoulder. Bob missed his parents. And he wondered what the hell he was doing in California.

24

The next morning Bob found Adelman and his team already deeply buried in documents at 9:00.

"So," Bob said. "Show me."

Adelman showed him, and there was no doubt. Starting about six months before, Berkman was depositing large sums in a bank account identified only by number.

"And this looks like a Swiss bank account number?"

"Absolutely. As I say, I've seen it before."

"Under what sort of circumstances?" Bob wasn't sure he wanted to hear the answer, but felt compelled to ask.

"Well. Tax avoidance. Or hiding illegally obtained funds. Or. . . ."

"Or?"

"Or planning a divorce. Often before the spouse knows."

The word hung in the area like California smog.

"Oh." It was all Bob could think of to say for a moment.

California was a community property state; unless there was a prenup, all assets were evenly divided in a divorce. That, Bob knew, would be a good motive for squirreling away money somewhere no one could find it.

Bob pulled himself out of his fog. It was only 9:15 but he felt tired.

"Can you check his tax returns, see if there's a possible explanation?"

"Yes, we're doing that right now." Adelman motioned to his assistants. "Should have an answer soon."

"Right. Thanks."

Bob walked over to Duane's office.

"Oh, Jesus! How much are we talking about?"

"About three million."

"That's a lot of money." Duane started fiddling around with his glasses. "I can't imagine tax fraud, or something like that. For one thing, when Amy ran for mayor, the local press put Berkman's business under a microscope. And she disclosed their tax returns."

"Everyone might have missed this, and it hasn't been going on for very long." Bob hesitated. "And if it's not something to do with the business, then we have to consider . . ."

Duane took off his glasses and gave him a skeptical look, but Bob decided to press on. In for a penny, in for a pound.

"We have to consider the possibility that Sam was planning a divorce. Or at least seriously considering it. We'll have to look into the marriage, their personal lives."

Duane didn't say anything for a minute. Bob felt a trickle of sweat under his armpits.

"Okay," Duane finally said. "I'll tell Fred. You talk to Perez, see if they have caught a scent of any marital trouble." He paused. "This case is like a rock. You turn it over and you don't know what's underneath."

After Bob went back to his office, Duane got up, closed the door after him, and made a call.

"Boss, we've got a big problem."

25

Back in his office, Bob left a message for Detective Perez, who was out. He tried to go back to his bar exam prep, but his mind was racing.

Was Berkman some kind of criminal? A tax cheat? Or was a divorce in the offing? Was Sam seeing someone else? Bob remembered a neighbor of his parents in Connecticut who was a marriage counselor. One summer night when his parents had invited her and her husband over for dinner, Bob remembered her saying that the three main causes of divorce were adultery, empty nest syndrome, and kitchen renovation. She meant it as a joke, but, after everyone laughed, she said there was a lot of truth in it.

Well, the Berkman kids were young, so the nest was still full. And they were so rich they would rent or buy someplace else if they were renovating their house, and not be inconvenienced in the least. Sam developed property, that would have been super-easy.

As he was lost in thought, Perez returned his call.

"What's up, kid?"

Bob told him the latest and asked if they had picked up any sign of marital trouble.

"No, at least not yet. But we're still digging. Don't forget we see the therapist at two o'clock. She'd be the one to ask."

Bob went back to his binders and was able to concentrate just enough to know what he was reading. Around 11:00 Cathy stuck her head in to say the accountants needed to see him.

Adelman was shuffling papers when Bob walked in.

"So. We've been through the files sent by Cunningham's lawyer. The numbers there track what we've seen in Berkman's files. Cunningham invested ten million dollars. It's clear he expected it to be used for a project in Chula Vista; there's no mention of Oceanside. But, as I said, the contract only refers to San Diego county. Previous investments were smaller, and earned a good return, an average of seven percent."

Bob was taking notes.

"And so far, we're not seeing any evidence of tax fraud or anything like that. The money Berkman put in that Swiss account is what he earned from his last major project, a new development in Lake Forest. It was properly reported."

"Where is Lake Forest?"

"Up in Orange County. Just east of Laguna Beach. Very upscale. We'll keep digging but that's the story so far."

"What about Lincoln Savings? Anything weird there?"

"No. Everything is documented, the contracts are standard, nothing illegal or even questionable. I showed some of the contracts to Duane. All kosher."

Bob was disappointed, in a way; he had hoped there might have been funny business with Charles Keating. From what he had read in the news, Keating often operated outside the law; he might be capable of arranging a murder.

Bob thanked Adelman and went back to his office. When Jennifer called to ask how he was getting on, Bob said he had a few questions and invited her to lunch. They met at the same restaurant in Hillcrest and waited a few minutes for a table outside. Bob was relieved to get out of the office.

After they ordered, Bob asked her if she had any sense of the Berkman marriage.

"Hmm, interesting question." Jennifer thought for a moment or two. "When Amy first went into local politics, Sam was always by her side, and they often paraded their kids in front of the cameras, despite the kids being really young. It was kind of sickening, to tell you the truth."

"Too much apple pie?"

"Yeah. Way too much mommy and daddy. As time went on, though, they did that less and less. And Sam wasn't at Amy's side at community events nearly as much. Or hardly at all, really."

"Interesting. This is off the record, but did you ever pick up any sense of trouble in the marriage?"

Jennifer hesitated. "Completely off the record?"

"Absolutely."

"There were some rumors that Amy always had her eye on hot young men."

"Oh?" Bob was taken aback.

"Yeah. Nothing anyone could put their finger on, but yeah. Definitely. Her aides always seemed to be these gorgeous young hunks who could have been models."

"I see."

"Of course, that's true of at least a third of the guys around here. All these cute marines and sailors running around, and a lot of them stick around after they leave the service. They don't go back to Nebraska."

Bob laughed. "Yes, I've noticed. What about Sam?"

"Well, you know, what's sauce for the goose . . ."

"Yeah. Lots of sauce in San Diego." Bob looked around; most of the lunch crowd was gorgeous, and several of the men were wearing as little as possible. All the women were thin and well-dressed, and everyone looked like they went to the gym regularly.

For a moment, he surprised himself by wondering if he or Marcus would ever be tempted to stray. Neither of them had, he was sure of that. Bob knew that most long-term gay couples had open relationships, but he had talked about it with Marcus, and both wanted monogamy when they first got together, for many reasons, not the least of which was HIV.

But that was a while ago, and here they were in a new environment, with countless young servicemen running around. And he knew he had been so busy with law school and the Law Review and now the job that he had been neglecting Marcus, maybe just a little. He felt a pang of guilt, and a split second of worry.

"Now, down to business," Jennifer said. "How's your prep going?"

26

After lunch, with a little time to kill, Bob strolled around the Hillcrest business district. It was clearly the gay ghetto, with gift shops and bars displaying rainbow flags and lots of people out and about. It was a beautiful, sunny day and there were gay men everywhere, some of them casually cruising, though it was the middle of the day.

He wandered into a decrepit little bookstore with a blue door that had a nice, East Coast feel and glanced at a few titles. He saw a book on California politics and bought it; he realized he hadn't picked up a book, other than Jennifer's binders, since arriving in California. He missed reading.

Around 1:45 p.m. he went to meet Perez and Duane at the office of Sam Berkman's therapist in Mission Hills, a wealthy neighborhood just to the west of Hillcrest. The address he had been given was a large private home with an immaculate front lawn. A discreet wrought iron sign at the front door pointed to "The offices of Dr. Marcia Aaron" around the side of the house.

Perez and Duane were waiting on a small patio. There were chairs but no one sat. At exactly 2:00 o'clock a side door opened and a very attractive woman around forty, with long blond hair, came out, introduced herself, and invited them into her office. She was wearing a stunning peach-colored suit, a white silk blouse, and very high heels.

As they were arranging themselves on the couch and chairs, Aaron offered coffee, which they all declined.

"I should say at the outset," she said before anyone else had a chance to speak, "that I cannot tell you anything specific about my work with Mr. Berkman. As I'm sure you know, our relationship is covered by doctor-patient confidentiality, and protected by law."

"Even though Mr. Berkman was murdered?" Perez asked in his Dana Andrews voice.

"Yes, absolutely. Imagine how my other patients would feel if I violated someone's trust."

Duane responded. "We certainly understand that. But can you tell us, how long have you been treating Mr. Berkman? How often did you meet?"

"We had been working together for roughly a year. We met twice a week."

"And how did Mr. Berkman come to you?"

"He had been given my name by his physician."

Perez spoke up. "Was he taking any medication?"

"I shouldn't answer that."

"Well, Doctor," Perez said, "we could subpoena his medical and insurance records."

Aaron hesitated. "He was taking a low dose of Paxil, an anti-depressant."

"Did you prescribe it for him?"

"I had referred him to a psycho-pharmacologist who recommended this particular drug."

Perez continued. "Did you consider Mr. Berkman a danger to himself, or to others?"

"No, absolutely not. As I'm sure you know, if he had been, I would have been under a legal obligation to speak to the authorities."

Perez continued. "If you have any idea who might have murdered him, you also have an obligation to tell us that."

Duane didn't think that was true if she had only a suspicion, but Aaron responded by saying she had no idea whatsoever. Duane then asked whether she could give them a general idea of the issues that brought him to therapy.

"I'm afraid that question is out of bounds. Is there anything else?"

Bob spoke up, again surprising everyone else in the room. He realized he was doing that a lot lately.

"Was there any sign that the Berkman marriage was troubled?"

Bob got what he was aiming for—a reaction. The doctor's demeanor changed immediately. "That is completely out of bounds," she said icily.

After a moment, Duane glanced at Perez and Bob and then thanked her for her time. They all stood.

As they walked to their cars, Perez looked at Bob and said, "Another smart move, kid."

Duane agreed. "Yeah. Clearly the marriage was an issue. But we don't know really know how. I mean, anyone in therapy is going to talk about their marriage."

Bob wasn't so sure it wasn't a useful reaction. "I don't know. Her tone changed. So did her body language. Her expression. I think maybe the question touched a nerve."

Duane turned to Perez. "Have you guys uncovered anything about the marriage?"

Perez said no, so far nothing, and got into his car. He looked uncomfortable and seemed to want to get away as quickly as possible.

Bob was trying to organize his thoughts about that when

Duane told him the accountants wanted to see him when they got back to the office.

27

On the drive back to the office, Bob tried to put the pieces of the case together, but, like the jigsaw puzzles that used to frustrate him as a child, the pieces weren't fitting. His older brother always finished the puzzles.

He still didn't think Cunningham was likely to be the killer. Between the Swiss bank account, what he had heard from Jennifer, and Dr. Aaron's reaction to his question, he was beginning to suspect the Berkman marriage might be important to the case . . . but how?

And how did Otley fit in? They needed to know more, much more. Maybe there was an innocent explanation for all of it. And maybe Amy needed to put her family in front of the cameras at first—to get elected, as Jennifer had said— but, after that it didn't really matter so much.

But Bob's gut was telling him they were going to have to ask the mayor some uncomfortable questions, and his heart sank at the idea.

And then a thought popped into his head, a notion that had been forming in the back of his mind for days.

What if the mayor killed her husband?

A chill ran down his spine.

He thought back to what they knew about the day of the murder. The mayor was at home, with her kids, probably with a nanny or maid or both. Sam was due home; there was that note on his desk at the office. When Sam didn't come home, Amy was driven to Los Angeles for that reception.

Her movements were accounted for. She was not the murderer.

But she wouldn't be the first jealous wife to have her husband killed by someone else. And she had access to plenty of security people, and plenty of money.

Bob pulled over to a curb and killed his engine.

But was she a jealous wife? They didn't even know if the divorce was real. It was just a theory—pure speculation.

And besides, how could a mayor think she could get away with murder? She'd have to pay someone to do it. That would leave a cash trail. And it would open her up to blackmail. She'd know that. Too dangerous.

And the cops haven't picked up any sign of trouble in the marriage. At least not yet. And if the marriage was imploding, she could divorce Sam. Divorce didn't mean political death anymore, even for Republicans. Everyone knew that.

Just look at Reagan.

Bob told himself it was all too far-fetched, that he had watched too many noir films from the fifties, full of scheming women with dirty little secrets. This was real life, not the movies, even if it was Southern California.

He started his engine.

28

Back at the courthouse Bob went straight to Adelman's office.

Adelman was finishing a doughnut. He wiped his chin and said, "Okay, Sam did pay taxes on the money he deposited in

Switzerland. There was a lot of fancy footwork involved in how the income was reported over time, but nothing illegal. My guess is, he had a very savvy tax advisor."

"I see."

"That's the bad news, if you're looking for a smoking gun. So to speak. The good news is that we've uncovered a series of arguments with a contractor who was very angry. The arguments escalated over time."

"Oh?"

"Yes, Amalgamated Roofing. The owner is Edgar Rosenblatt. The broad outlines are clear. They were tardy in getting some roofing finished a few years back, Berkman was not happy, and delayed payment. Subsequent contracts had a penalty clause if work wasn't completed on time. Rosenblatt was upset about that, but he did take the jobs. Then Berkman invoked the penalties. Rosenblatt wrote some very nasty letters." He pushed a bunch of papers over to Bob.

Bob scanned the letters, and they were, in fact, very angry.

"And," Adelman added, "Rosenblatt was owed a substantial sum when Berkman was killed. Not clear why payment was withheld."

"How much are we talking about?"

"Around four-hundred-fifty thousand. I'd say that's a lot of money to your average roofing company. It's a cash-flow business. And now, I imagine, that money may be tied up in the estate."

"I wonder why they continued to do business with each other."

"Good question. Maybe Amalgamated were the cheapest around."

"Could be. But we should definitely look into this."

Bob made copies of some of the correspondence and

took them to Duane, who agreed it was an interesting lead. He called Perez, who said he'd set up an interview with Rosenblatt and, if necessary, get a subpoena.

Bob spent the rest of the day on bar exam prep, nearly falling asleep once or twice. Around 5:30 he was ready to leave for the day when Cathy stuck her head in. Bob noticed that today's scarf was orange, not a good color for her.

"Fred wants to see you."

"Now?"

"Now."

When Bob got to the DA's office, he was surprised that Duane wasn't there.

This can't be good, he said to himself.

He stood up as straight as he could.

Fred was shuffling papers on his desk and did not look up. He kept opening and closing his left fist.

Bob stood in front of the desk and waited.

"I understand you think we need to delve into the Berkman marriage." The DA's tone was all business, zero warmth.

Bob knew he was about to be told off, and made a split-second decision to fight back. He opted for a strategy recommended by a lawyer he had worked for in the summer after his second year of law school: Answer a challenge with a challenge, a question with a question.

"Don't you?"

"Not really. What's your thinking?" Fred finally looked up.

"Sam Berkman was in therapy. He had recently deposited a great deal of money into a Swiss bank account. One scenario that could explain those two things is that the marriage was troubled in some way and Sam was planning a divorce. Or at least considering it."

"Lots of people are in therapy and have Swiss bank accounts. Both perfectly legal."

"Of course. But how many of those people get murdered? *Something* was going on that got Sam Berkman killed."

"I'm really not interested in the Berkman marriage. Our job is to find and prosecute a murderer, not drag people through the mud."

"I understand that. But still we need as complete a picture as possible of the victim's life at the time of the murder. Don't we?"

"Of course, yes," his boss answered testily. Almost immediately he added, "To the extent we need to. But be careful about the questions you ask or the theories you suggest. If the press gets hold of the fact that someone in the DA's office thinks a divorce was in the offing, they will go nuts. We could end up hurting the career of a rising political star for no good reason. If we do that, without justification, there will be hell to pay."

"How would the press find out? I haven't discussed this with anyone outside the office."

Fred paused. "Are you sure?"

Bob's mind was racing. Jennifer? Or was Fred just assuming a young, green ADA couldn't possibly be discreet about a case like this? Or was this a preemptive warning?

"Yes, I'm sure." Bob decided to do preemptive damage control of his own. "I asked a local attorney her general impressions of the Berkman marriage. A perfectly natural question when someone is murdered. I said nothing about the bank account or a divorce."

"I see."

"And the police are also looking into Berkman's private life. It was the police who got the information about his therapist and wanted to interview her."

"Yes, I know."

"If you want me off the case, sir, I'll be glad to step back."

"Well, no." Fred's tone softened and he shook his head.

Bob's strategy was working. And he was also getting angry. Was Jennifer a spy? If not, and Fred was just fishing, why was he fishing?

"Or resign altogether. I'm sure I can find another job."

"There's no need to go overboard. Just be careful."

Bob knew he should probably stop talking; he had made his point. But he was thinking of something his father once told his brother: A good lawyer makes his intentions clear to his client. If the client doesn't like it, walk away. The DA wasn't Bob's client, exactly, but the DA's office as a whole had a client.

The public. And if the DA didn't want all the facts, he wasn't doing the job he needed to do for his client.

"I am careful," Bob said. "But if you're telling us not to look into the Berkman marriage, I could not accept that, and I can't imagine the police would either. If those are your orders, I'd have no choice but to leave."

"Look. There's no need for that. You can look into it. Just be careful, and go no further than you need to."

Bob nodded. "Certainly."

"Have a good evening."

The dismissal was clear. The DA went back to the paperwork on his desk, and Bob walked out feeling almost proud of himself; the thought crossed his mind to wonder what his father would think.

29

He went to his office and sat down. He willed himself to be calm. Slowly his breathing returned to normal.

It didn't make any sense. What was the DA doing? Was he really just concerned about rumors hitting the press? Didn't that happen often enough in sensational cases? Amy Berkman was mayor. If she wanted to deny trouble in the marriage—if it hit the press—all she had to do was put out a statement, or call a press conference.

And how could the DA ignore the facts that were coming to light? A Swiss bank account. Therapy. A mysterious bequest in Sam's will to someone with a shady past.

Was Jennifer really spying on him? Is that why she was brought in as his bar coach? If that was the case, then the sooner he quit this job, the better.

Bob gathered his things and drove home. He found a note from Marcus. "Took the dog, hate Kansas. Love, Dorothy."

Bob laughed out loud. He stripped, leaving his clothes where they dropped, and drew a bath. He almost never took baths but wanted nothing more than to soak in hot water. While the tub was filling he poured himself a scotch.

He sank himself into the tub, closed his eyes, and sipped his drink. He had been dozing for a few minutes when he heard Marcus come home.

"Good God. What are you doing?"

"It's called a bath. We take them here on planet Earth."

Marcus laughed.

"I'm trying to forget today happened."

"Bad day?"

"Well, it's only my first week, but I've already been called on the carpet by the big boss. Sort of."

"Oh, God. Why?"

"I can't tell you."

"Well get dressed, there's nothing for dinner. We're going out."

Bob did as he was told.

While he was dressing, he called to Marcus, who was in his study. "Let's go somewhere near the water. I want to stare at the ocean."

They drove to Ocean Beach, a funky neighborhood where, as one of their guidebooks put it, the 1960s were still going strong. They found a beachside fish house with an unobstructed, picture-postcard view. They didn't talk much, just stared at the waves, the expanse of the sea, the mesmerizing vista of the setting sun as it turned the sky pink and orange with a stripe of green above the horizon.

After dinner they walked onto the Ocean Beach pier, which extended so far out that you could see the back of the waves as they approached the shore. Watching and listening to the waves was hypnotic. At the very end were a few fishermen, and down in the surf several surfers in wet suits, paddling around, waiting for the last big one of the day.

"Is it the case? Is it getting messy?" Marcus asked as gently as he could.

"Yeah. At least, I think so. I'm not sure anyone else does."

Marcus could tell Bob didn't want to talk about it, or couldn't. He changed the subject. "Looking at the waves like this, I can understand the appeal of surfing. Even the small waves have such power. To be a part of that in some way. . . ." His voice drifted off.

Bob closed his eyes and inhaled. "Yes. But it's dangerous.

It must be."

"I suppose. Like your job."

Bob smiled. It was getting chilly, so they wandered back to their car. On the way home they stopped for coffee at a little place in Hillcrest and shared a piece of carrot cake. By the time they made it back to the house, Bob was sleepy, but at least he felt in control again. At least a little.

Marcus put on Ella Fitzgerald, and they snuggled on the couch. Then the phone rang. Before Marcus could get up to answer it, Bob said, "Let it ring."

30

The next morning he really didn't want to get out of bed, but when he heard Marcus in the kitchen and smelled French toast, he smiled with anticipation.

He made it to the office by 9:00, and Duane caught him in the hallway and followed him into his office. Bob waited for him to start the conversation.

"I hear you got your first dose of the real Fred last night."

"You might say that."

Bob sat.

"Don't take it personally. This case is really weighing on him, it's so high profile. And he knows and likes the mayor." Duane took off his glasses.

"I see."

Bob had decided he was going to be careful about what he did and did not say to Duane, to Cathy—or Jennifer. At least for the time being, he wouldn't confront Jennifer. If she was a spy, she'd only report back; if not, he'd offend one of the few people he knew in town.

"Although Fred plays his cards close to his chest," Duane was saying, "I think he and Amy are more or less in sync politically, even though they're in different parties. Both see themselves as part of the responsible middle."

"I can understand that."

"And . . ." Duane hesitated.

Bob finished his sentence for him. ". . . and if we mess this up, it could cost Fred politically. The stakes are high for him. He's relatively young."

"Anyway, I tried calling you last night. You and the cops have an interview with that contractor at ten. At police HQ. And then at noon, you're meeting with Sam's lunch partner from the day of the murder."

"Okay."

"Then take the rest of the day studying for the bar. Unless something else breaks."

Duane left, and Bob got up and poured himself a cup of coffee from the communal pot in the small kitchenette down the hall. He sat and did nothing until it was time to drive to the police headquarters.

He made his way to the detectives' squad room. When Perez saw him he joined him in the doorway.

"Bobbitt's home sick," he said.

So neither of us will have our sidekicks, Bob thought to himself as they walked together to one of the interview rooms. As usual, Bob stationed himself behind the mirror.

A few minutes after 10:00 Perez ushered Edgar Rosenblatt into the interview room. He hadn't brought an attorney. Rosenblatt was around sixty, well dressed and composed. He had a Woody Allen-type face, and it was hard to square his mild appearance with the vitriol in his letters.

It turned out Rosenblatt had been working in Orange County the day of the murder, at least an hour's drive from San Diego, giving estimates on various job sites and consulting a local crew.

"I know why you wanted to speak to me. Those letters. Maybe some of them were over the top. But Sam could be slow making payment. Very slow. My business depends on cash flow. There are heavy outlays for equipment and supplies." He paused, then continued. "And Sam is a distant cousin. Was. So I didn't need to pull punches."

Though as surprised by this information as Bob, Perez displayed nothing beyond a brief glance toward the mirror.

Rosenblatt had written down a list of the people he had seen the day of the murder, along with the times. If the list was accurate, there was no way he could have been the killer.

Perez asked the questions one would expect, why did Sam Berkman withhold payment and so forth, and took notes, but it was obvious Rosenblatt wasn't the murderer. Perez thanked him for his time and asked him to notify him if he was going to be out of town.

"If you have any further need of me," Rosenblatt said, "here's the name of my lawyer. Please contact him." He handed Perez a business card.

Bob walked back with Perez to his desk.

"Not our guy," Bob said as he sat down next to the desk.

"No. We'll check his alibis, but no. He didn't do it."

"So what's your thinking so far?" Bob asked.

"Hard to say. I suppose it's possible Cunningham hired someone to do it, but I kinda doubt it."

"What about the marriage?" Bob asked. "Anything there?"

"There doesn't seem to be. We've talked to the people who work for them in the house, including a maid who lives there, and some of the mayor's staff. A few neighbors and people in their social circle. No real dirt. Of course, that doesn't mean there isn't something there, but so far, nothing."

Bob wondered why he or someone else from the DA's office hadn't sat in on those interviews, but he let it pass for the moment.

"And what about the money in Switzerland?"

The detective took a long gulp of coffee. "Well, he wasn't hiding it from the tax man. Maybe it was just a safe place to park some cash."

"I suppose. Any other suspects?"

"We haven't found any yet. I was kinda hoping your accountants would come up with more."

"I know they're trying."

Perez picked up some papers on his desk, as if to say, I need to get to work. Bob thanked him and asked him the details of the Cunningham interview.

"We meet him at this house in Carlsbad at two on Saturday." Perez gave him the address.

"Kid, let me give you some advice. Keep on the good side of Fred Stevens. I've seen him fire a lot of ADAs lately."

Bob nodded and asked about the noon meeting with the lunch partner, Cecil Richardson. Perez told him he didn't need to be there, but Bob said he would be.

31

They had arranged to meet Richardson at the La Jolla Country Club, where, he had said, he spent every morning playing golf.

Bob met the detectives in the parking lot. Richardson was waiting for them in the bar, sipping a drink, dressed in bright green slacks and a white polo shirt. Bob had always wondered why golfers favored such garish colors.

Richardson was a well-preserved man of about sixty; he looked like someone whose life had been eased at every step by abundant money. According to Duane he had made his fortune on the stock market in New York by the time he was forty, then moved to La Jolla to live the good life.

"Gentlemen," he said, standing up, "can I offer you a mimosa? Or perhaps just orange juice? They make it freshly squeezed here, from their own oranges."

They all shook their heads as they sat down on comfortable leather sofas.

"So I assume you want to talk to me about poor Sam Berkman."

"Yes," Perez said, "it turns out you were one of the last people to see him alive."

"Yes. Horrible thing. Just horrible."

"Can you tell us, why were you meeting?" Perez asked.

"I was considering an investment in some of Sam's property developments."

"Can you be specific?"

"Actually, no. We didn't discuss any particular project, although he mentioned a development in Oceanside. But this was a first meeting. I just wanted to get a sense of how Sam worked, who he was."

"And what would have been the size of your investment?" Bob asked.

"Somewhere north of two million."

Perez was taking notes. "How did Sam approach you?" he asked.

"Actually, I approached him. I heard about him from Maude."

That took a moment to sink in.

"Maude Cunningham?" Perez asked, doing his best to hide his surprise.

"Yes. I've known Maudey a long time. We're involved in some of the same charities."

"And how," Perez asked, "did you come to discuss Sam Berkman?"

"It was by chance. I was at a reception at Maude's home, in Hancock Park." Hancock Park, Bob knew, was the home of many old money families in Los Angeles.

"Go on."

"She asked me, rather out of the blue, if I had any cash that needed investing. And as it happened, I did. She said Jamey had invested with Sam and it might be worth looking into."

"That would be James Cunningham, Maude's son?"

"Right."

"And when was this?" Bobbitt asked.

"A few months ago."

"Anything else you can tell us about your encounter with Mr. Berkman?" Perez asked.

"Not really. It was quite straightforward. I thanked him and we said good-bye."

"And were you going to make the investment?"

"I was mulling it over. I was planning to talk to Jamey, but then Sam died, and that was that."

"So you never talked to James Cunningham?"

"No."

"Can you say," Perez asked, "if Mr. Berkman seemed upset or especially worried that day?"

"Very hard to say, I was meeting him for the first time.

But no, he seemed quite calm, very polished."

Perez glanced at Bob, who had no questions, and thanked Richardson for his time.

"Not at all. I hope you catch the killer. He seemed like a nice guy."

As they reached their cars, Perez said, more to himself than to Bob, "Why would Cunningham's mother be shilling for Berkman?"

Bob turned back. "Maybe her son was worried about his own investment and she wanted to help him out."

"Could be," Perez said. "I'll report in to the chief."

On his drive back downtown, Bob thought about what they had just heard. It reinforced his sense that James Cunningham was not the likely murderer. The man was worried about his investment and trying to protect it by bringing others in. Killing Sam wouldn't accomplish that.

He did find it amusing that the matriarch of an incredibly wealthy family was giving investment advice. He was beginning to think the Cunninghams were much like some of the old aristocratic families in the English and French novels he'd loved in college, wealthy and above it all on the surface, devoting themselves to high society and charity, looking down on the middle and lower classes—but, in private, keeping a cold eye on cash flow.

32

Bob plopped himself down at this desk and stared at his bar exam binders. What he really needed, he decided, was to talk everything over with his father. Not just the murder, but the office drama. Especially the office drama.

And then he remembered Otley in New York. A few days ago they were thinking of sending him to interview Otley. If it happened, he could combine a trip to do the interview with a quick visit to his parents' house in Danbury.

He walked over to Duane's office and told him the roofer wasn't the murderer, filled him in on Richardson, and asked about Otley.

"Yeah. Otley."

"Maybe I should take a trip to New York."

"First let me find out if David has told Otley about the bequest."

"David?"

"David Sanders. Sam's lawyer and the executor of the estate. Our travel budget is tight, so we try to do advanced purchase fares. In the meantime we ask the mayor next week if she knows him. Might save us the trip."

Bob went back to his office, and just as he started on the binders, Marcus called from his office at UCSD.

"You remember Jim and Arlene from dinner, right? They invited us over to their place tonight. Just us, very casual, they said. In fact, their freezer broke down and they have steaks they need to use before they go bad."

Bob laughed. "Sure, what time?"

"They said come around seven. I'll go straight from here." Marcus gave him the address in La Jolla.

Bob started in on the Contracts binder and let out a sigh.

At 2:30, Billy Lewis, the friendliest ADA, stuck his head in and asked Bob if he'd had lunch; Bob realized he hadn't.

"Do you always eat this late?" Bob asked.

Billy laughed. "On busy days, sometimes."

Bob hoped Billy wasn't going to give him another lecture,

but said he'd be glad to have lunch. Anything to get away from the binders.

They drove to the Crest Café in Hillcrest, where Billy seemed to know everyone who worked there. It was the kind of place Bob loved, a simple neighborhood diner, still quite busy at 3:00. It was just down the block from a gay bar, The Brass Rail, that seemed to be busy as well.

"So," Billy asked, "how are you settling in?"

"Well . . ." Bob didn't know what to say.

"Baptism by fire?"

"Yes." They both smiled.

"I hear you stood up to the boss. Good for you."

"Jesus, does everyone in the office know?"

"Pretty much." Billy laughed. "First rule of the DA's office—there are no secrets. Except maybe the ones Fred keeps himself."

"So, did I do the right thing?"

"Absolutely. Start out strong. Only way with him. He may not like it right off the bat, but he will come to respect you. If he thinks you're a wimp, eventually he'll get rid of you. It's fatal for a prosecutor."

Bob let that sink in, then asked, "Do you know the Berkmans?"

"I've met them. Don't know them at all. A power couple, as they say. Both very ambitious. For different things."

"Will Amy run for Cranston's Senate seat?"

"Wouldn't surprise me at all. And if she does . . ." Billy hesitated.

"If she does . . ." Bob prompted.

"If she does, and wins, it wouldn't surprise anyone if Fred ran for mayor."

"You don't say."

33

The talk turned to other things, and after lunch they headed back to the office. There was a note from Cathy about the Cunningham meeting the next afternoon.

Bob's mind was racing once again.

Amy goes to the Senate, and Fred runs for mayor. Quite a plan. No wonder he wants the heat on Cunningham, not Amy. He doesn't want anything to come out that might conceivably hurt Amy's career. His own path depended on her moving up.

"My, my," he muttered out loud.

He decided to take the rest of the afternoon off.

On a whim, he drove back to Ocean Beach and watched the surfers from the pier. The waves were strong and there were more surfers than there had been the evening before. Then he strolled around the Ocean Beach business strip and bought a cup of coffee, trying not to think about the case. From a bench he watched the people passing by, surfers, a few families, almost everyone wearing bathing suits. He closed his eyes and smelled the ocean.

He looked at his watch. He didn't have time to stop back at home, so he wandered around a bit more and then headed out to meet Marcus at the Stewarts.

It was the tail-end of rush hour, and traffic was heavy as Bob made his way up to La Jolla for the second time that day.

He remembered that La Jolla had been described to them as San Diego's equivalent of Beverly Hills. As Bob got off the freeway and made his way up Mount Soledad, he could see why—huge houses, with Soledad providing views of the ocean. He rolled down the windows and inhaled the sea air. It was funny; he thought, that driving nearly the same route that morning, he'd been preoccupied with the case and hardly noticed where he was.

When he and Marcus had first visited San Diego, they'd looked at a couple of houses in La Jolla, but the prices were absurd. They couldn't understand why the state had decided to build a university campus near prime real estate, and couldn't imagine that very many students, or staff for that matter, could afford to live nearby. Someone explained to them that the campus grew up around the Scripps Institute of Oceanography, which had been founded early in the twentieth century when there was almost nothing at all around it. There had also been a military base near Scripps during World War II, and the rest of the campus occupied the space of the base starting around 1960. Some departments, they learned, were still housed in what had been military barracks.

The Stewarts lived in a modern house on Inspiration Drive; Bob wondered if the town fathers named it in the hope of attracting professors. The house looked like it had been built in the 1960s.

When he rang the doorbell, Jim opened it; Marcus was standing behind him, drink in hand. They went into a large living room with a wall of windows that offered a panoramic view of Mission Bay to the south. The house was deceptive from the front; it was built into a hill, and huge.

Jim poured Bob a glass of wine, and after a moment Arlene came in from the kitchen with a tray of nibbles. They were delicious, though neither Bob nor Marcus had any idea what they were.

They settled on couches, and after a while a golden retriever came bounding in and made straight for the guests, demanding pats and ear scratches.

"That's Zelda. Named for Zelda Fitzgerald. This one is less crazy. A bit."

Bob told them about his brother and sister-in-law's dog. "We're going to take a puppy," he said.

"That's wonderful!" Jim exclaimed. "It'll be a handful, but you'll love her. Or him. Goldens are the most wonderful dogs in the world. They love you no matter what. But they're not watchdogs. We were burgled once and I'm sure Zelda wagged her tail and led the guy straight to the silver."

Everyone laughed and, as if on cue, Zelda settled in front of Bob, resting her head on his knee.

They chatted idly until Arlene excused herself to put the steaks on the grill, and after ten minutes or so she called everyone to the outside table on the deck off the dining room. It, too, had a view of the bay.

"That's quite a view," Marcus said.

"Yes, we never get tired of it. We're very lucky. We got here early enough."

As they ate he told them some of the history of UCSD, how it had started as a science-focused campus and how the medical school still called the shots.

When the dinner was done and it was getting chilly, Arlene suggested they take coffee and dessert—homemade peach pie, still warm from the oven—in the living room.

Jim asked Bob how he was settling in with the DA.

"Well, he takes some getting used to."

"I can imagine. We've met him a few times," Arlene said. "Ambitious."

"So I gather," Bob said.

Bob recalled the conversation about the Berkmans that they'd had at the restaurant in Hillcrest. He decided to probe a bit. His hosts seemed well plugged in to the local scene.

"Tell me," Bob said, "off the record, have you ever run across the Cunningham family?"

"Well," Jim said, pouring out brandy, "they're loaded, and socially prominent. The patriarch made a huge fortune early in the century, mostly by buying up land, and the family became very, very wealthy. Probably the most socially connected family in Los Angeles, if you take the long view. Over the years, they gave a lot of money to UC. I think one of them has a beach house down here."

"Do you know which one?" Bob tried to sound casual.

"One of the younger ones, I think. We met him once at a concert, didn't we, honey?"

"Yes," she said. "At the Chamber Music Society. John. No, James, I think his name was. He was with a stunning-looking woman. He was polite but clearly a snob."

"I've always been curious about old families like that," Marcus said, thinking of ways to gather more information for Bob without being too obvious about it. "What generation would he be?"

"Third, I think," Jim said.

"And what does the third generation of a family like that do? Is the fortune still intact?"

"Hard to say. The patriarch, William, had many children with two different wives. And of course each of them had families of their own. They lost a lot during the Depression, but not everything. Families with that kind of money don't ever lose everything, as far as I can tell," he added with a cynical laugh. "At any rate, I don't think James works, or needs to, or wants to. Was that your impression, hon?"

"Well, yes." Arlene said. "They're not the kind of old-money family that run banks or are three generations of lawyers. He seemed to be something of a jet-setter. But we only talked to him for a few minutes."

"If you're interested, I've got a book on twentieth century LA that talks about the family," Jim said.

Marcus glanced at Bob. "Sure. I'd love to borrow it."

When he brought the book from the library, Bob and Marcus thanked their hosts, said they'd have them over to Normal Heights as soon as the house was put together, and said their good nights.

As they walked to their separate cars, Marcus handed Bob the book.

Bob smiled. "You'd make a very good spy."

34

Bob sat up most of the night reading about the Cunninghams. It was quite a story, and, in many ways, he realized, it was the story of modern Southern California. The patriarch, William, moved to Los Angeles from a farming community in Nebraska after serving in the Navy and being discharged in Long Beach, just south of LA. He became a reporter and married a woman from a well-to-do family; they used her inheritance to start buying land at the edge of the city and kept buying land as the city's edge moved farther and farther out. They perceived, rightly, that the San Fernando Valley, then farmland, was ripe for development.

Six months after his first wife died William married a woman from an even wealthier family, and they used her family money to buy up newspapers and local magazines. Over the years William fathered six children. The four boys went to Stanford or Princeton; the two girls, Vassar. One of the girls married an Illinois politician who became a senator.

The sons, like their father, were prescient about the future of the region. In the 1930s, they realized that America would inevitably be forced to fight European fascism, and they understood that the war would be mechanized, with the federal government supplying huge sums for ships and, especially, airplanes. They invested accordingly, and the region started to grow exponentially. They placed ads in newspapers all over the Midwest and Southeast, encouraging people to come to Southern California, the land of sunshine and oranges and plentiful jobs.

People came.

In the early 1980s, another generation of the family saw the future—computer technology—and again put their money in the right place.

Between the family's land wealth and its newspapers, it made and unmade politicians and molded Los Angeles city government to its liking. Generally nonpartisan, at times they supported Republicans, at times Democrats, so long as the horse they backed had economic policies favoring growth. They were moderate on social issues, and they enjoyed becoming philanthropists, endowing hospitals and cultural institutions up and down the state. They supported Ronald Reagan's rise to the governor's mansion and the White House.

When the book was published in 1975, the total wealth of all branches of the family was estimated to be $3 billion, although it was so diversified, so tied up in so many different enterprises, that it was difficult to make a precise estimate.

At 3:00 a.m., Bob started falling asleep as he read, and finally joined Marcus in bed. Marcus stirred and asked him if he had learned a lot.

"Oh yeah. Tons."

35

He slept until 10:00, then stumbled into the kitchen and grabbed coffee. Marcus came in from the yard, where he had been weeding the flower bed. At the moment it was just a patch of dirt in which they intended to plant flowers, although they were uncertain what would grow best in this climate.

"Tell me about the Cunningham family," Marcus said.

"Rich. Smart. Connected. Powerful."

"And one of them is connected to Berkman?" Marcus knew Bob had an interview that afternoon connected to the case.

"Connected loosely. Through investments."

"Hmm. I looked it up. There's a Cunningham on UC's Board of Regents. Probably one of them." Regents of the University of California, appointed by the governor, had charge of the whole sprawling, nine-campus system. Like everything in California, higher education was orders of magnitude larger than in most of the rest of the country.

"Interesting. I imagine they're on boards all over the state."

They had omelets and toast and strong coffee for brunch. After a shower Bob sat outside and looked over his notes on the case. He decided to leave early and visit Berkman's housing development in Oceanside; it was just north of Carlsbad, where the interview would take place.

It was Saturday and there wasn't much traffic. The sun was strong and the sky was a brilliant blue. Bob zipped up I-15, the inland freeway, which passed by the Naval Station at Miramar (more cute guys, he knew, like Tom Cruise in *Top Gun*) before it hit a sea of red tile roofs on suburban houses in locations with names like Black Mountain Ranch and Rancho Penasquitos.

Taking the Oceanside exit, he quickly found Mar Vista, the Berkman development: acres and acres of white stucco houses and condo buildings. The area was hilly, and he could see green yards and, with some of the larger houses, pools. He drove around.

Looking only at any individual house, Bob thought, it looked quite nice—spacious, clean, contemporary. But the overall impression was of uniformity, if not conformity— unending repetition of stucco buildings and red tile roofs, all lined up symmetrically on curving side streets with names like Orange Blossom Road. There weren't many trees and there wasn't much vegetation beyond the front rows of houses, closest to the main entrance, which had beautiful green lawns undoubtedly created with sod. Some houses were already occupied, with Toyotas and Hondas parked in the driveways; others were still being finished. Signs announced "Easy financing available. VA zero down."

The development as a whole gave Bob an uneasy feeling.

He glanced at his watch and realized he needed to get to Carlsbad. He drove west to the coast freeway, I-5, and quickly found the exit he needed.

36

As he neared the coast, Bob relaxed. Carlsbad felt like a real place, a funky beach town. The houses didn't match, and some were painted fanciful colors, pink or turquoise or yellow. There were mature eucalyptus trees. He saw the appeal of living in a town like this.

Closer to the ocean, the houses were larger, until right up against the water there were several estates sitting on a bluff.

Cunningham's house was the largest in the neighborhood: cream-colored stucco and stone with the requisite red tile roof, and too big for its lot. An open gate led to a long cobblestone driveway that bisected a yard landscaped with bushes and, it seemed, too many flowers. The scent hung in the air. Bob recognized Duane's car, and Perez's. There was also a Porsche Bob did not recognize. To the side was a four-car garage.

Looking at the overdone property, Bob remembered something his mother had once said. "There's nothing sadder," she said, "than rich people without taste."

He rang the doorbell and was admitted by a casually formal—or formally casual—butler in a black suit and a blue shirt, but no tie.

Bob found his colleagues waiting in a step-down sitting room with a wall of open glass doors revealing an unobstructed view of the ocean. The sound and smell of the waves was strong. Beyond the doors was a two-level terrace with steps leading down to white sand. A hot tub was visible on the upper deck. The floor was dark wood and the room was decorated simply but tastefully. There were a few small oriental rugs in reds and blues and furniture and chairs covered in what looked like white silk or linen. On one side an enormous fireplace was framed by books. Above the mantel hung a painting Bob thought might be a Picasso, or perhaps a Braque.

When the men had been seated by the butler, James Cunningham made what was clearly intended to be an entrance. He looked to be about 35, tall and slender, with wavy black hair and blue eyes. He had on white linen slacks and a dark blue polo shirt, and he was barefoot.

"Gentlemen. I'm Jim Cunningham."

The men all stood, and, as though choreographed, a maid, or perhaps a secretary, appeared out of nowhere with a tray holding teacups and cookies. She was an attractive woman in her twenties, Bob guessed. She offered all the guests tea and placed the plate of cookies on a coffee table. Duane and Bob accepted tea; Perez and Bobbitt did not.

"Will there be anything else, sir?"

"Would anyone like anything stronger than tea?" Cunningham asked. Then he answered his own question. "But you all are on duty. Foolish of me. Please, sit."

They did, and almost immediately Cunningham's lawyer appeared, with perfect timing, like his client.

Carter apologized for being late. "I was on the phone," he explained. He was dressed similarly to Cunningham, but his polo shirt was green and he was wearing sandals.

Bob wondered where rich Californians were taught what to wear.

Duane began, putting out a formal, official vibe.

"Thank you for seeing us."

Cunningham replied. "Not at all."

"Can you tell us about your relationship with Sam Berkman, and your meeting with him on July 7th?"

"Of course. I had met Sam a number of years ago at a political fundraiser for Amy. I was impressed with Amy and wound up being invited by her to various events. I got to know them socially, once at a dinner at their home in La Jolla."

Bobbitt was taking notes.

"And," Perez asked, "you invested in his building projects?"

"Yes. Initially, starting around two or three years ago, I invested small amounts, a million or so per project."

Bob noted that to Cunningham "a million or so" was a

"small amount." He couldn't suppress a smile.

"And did you earn a profit?"

"Yes. A quite respectable profit."

"And then?"

"And then Sam came to me about a year ago and suggested a larger investment for a development in Chula Vista. It seemed like a good bet. That area needed upscale housing. And I was looking for an opportunity."

"And," Duane asked, "you invested ten million?"

"Yes," Cunningham replied after sipping his tea, "something like that."

Again, the feigned nonchalance about money, no doubt well practiced over time.

"And you saw him at his office in Mission Valley," Perez asked, "on what turned out to be his last afternoon alive?"

"Yes."

"What was the nature of that conversation?"

"Well." Cunningham put down his tea, got up and went to a bar tucked away in a corner of the room, and poured himself a glass of sherry.

"To be frank, I was not happy that Sam had diverted some of my money to his project in Oceanside."

"Why was that?" Duane asked.

Carter spoke for his client. "Mr. Berkman had told Mr. Cunningham that his funds would be used in Chula Vista, not Oceanside."

"But," Perez said, "the contract did not specify that."

"True," Carter replied. "But Mr. Berkman made assurances."

"And why," Duane asked, "was the Oceanside development an undesirable investment? Please allow Mr. Cunningham to reply."

Bob was impressed that Duane shut down the lawyer, at least for the moment. Carter did not look pleased. He crossed his arms over his chest.

Cunningham took another swig of his sherry. The look on his face could only be described as patrician disdain.

"Oceanside is just north of here. I looked around the development. I was not impressed, and I knew the units were not selling well. I knew Sam had to go to some," here he searched for the right word, "disreputable sources for funds."

"By that," Duane asked, "do you mean Lincoln Savings?"

Cunningham's jaw tightened. "Yes. I had no interest in being mixed up in anything involving Lincoln Savings. I know how they operate." He let out a little laugh. "And now the whole country is learning."

"So you argued that afternoon?" Perez asked.

"Yes." Cunningham seemed to have no problem at all admitting that.

Perez continued. "Was there any resolution to the argument?"

Again, the lawyer answered. "No, there was not. Mr. Berkman argued that his actions fell within the terms of the contract, and, in a strictly legal sense, he was correct."

"So," Duane asked, "there was nothing that could be done?"

"Not unless we went to court and argued there was an oral contract," Carter replied. "And we decided against that."

Perez again. "Did Mr. Berkman seem unusually upset or worried that day?"

Cunningham replied with a sly smile. "Well, I think he knew that he would be receiving no more capital from me, and I imagine that was a worry. But beyond that, I couldn't say."

Everyone let that sink in.

"Where did you go after your meeting with Mr.

Berkman?" Perez asked.

"I drove back here. I took a swim and sat in the jacuzzi with a friend. Then we had dinner here."

"We'll need the name of that friend."

"Of course. Lucy Hargrove. And the staff was here, of course."

Hargrove's name was a surprise; the four men had met her briefly when she was Florence Russo's attorney.

Cunningham seemed to enjoy the look on their faces.

Finally Duane spoke. "I think that covers it. One more thing. Did Mr. Berkman offer you something to drink?"

"Yes, a small glass of sherry. I was driving, after all." He smiled again.

Perez gave Cunningham and Carter his card and pointed to Bobbitt, who was carrying a small case with fingerprint equipment.

"As we indicated, we need your fingerprints. It will only take a moment. Thank you again," Duane said. "And please do not leave Southern California without checking in with us, for the time being."

"Of course."

The butler reappeared and showed everyone to the door.

In the driveway, Perez said, under his breath, "That was one smooth character."

"No kidding," Duane said. "Post-mortem Monday morning at nine in Fred's office. In the meantime, Perez, check the fingerprints, and see if you can set up a meeting with Lucy Hargrove."

Perez nodded. After about fifteen minutes Bobbitt came out with the fingerprint kit, and the two of them drove off.

"What do you think?" Duane asked Bob as he was getting into his car.

"I think," Bob said, "old California money doesn't like mixing with the common folk. And he didn't murder Berkman."

37

Bob and Marcus spent the rest of the weekend relaxing and painting. They slept in on Sunday, and late in the afternoon they sat in the living room admiring their handiwork.

After a while Marcus said, "Maybe it should be white."

"No." Bob looked at him, not sure if he was serious or not. "Yellow's good. White is too . . . white."

Marcus laughed.

They rewarded themselves with dinner at California Cuisine. From their table on the patio they caught snippets of other conversations that mostly revolved around typical gay-San Diego topics—food, boyfriends, trysts, bars—except one comment from the next table expressing sympathy about "Amy and Sam." They clearly liked Amy; but when one of his tablemates said something about "Sammy," Bob considered asking if, and how well, they knew him. Or what they knew about him.

But he was tired of thinking about the Berkmans and whatever secrets they might have had.

After a shared chocolate tart and a short walk they were glad to head home. When the phone rang, Bob was tempted to ignore it, thinking it might be Duane or Cathy with more last-minute job needs. *Not tonight; not again*, he said to himself.

Marcus answered, and almost immediately grinned and

handed the phone to Bob. "We're parents!" he whispered.

Sophie now had four female and three male puppies, Bob learned from his brother, and they could choose the one they wanted very soon. When they hung up, Bob turned to Marcus, who said, "I guess we'll have to start saving for college. Just think how much fun it'll be. How domestic!"

Bob laughed. "Training him."

Marcus responded, "Taking him out for walks."

"Scooping poop out of the yard . . ."

They sat together on the couch, quietly hugging and smiling at one another. For a few blissful hours, they had forgotten about murder.

"Come on," said Marcus, "let's get to bed."

Neither one of them noticed the car parked across the street, or the man at the wheel who sat watching their house.

38

B ob woke up early and sat on the patio with a cup of strong coffee. He tried to prepare himself mentally for the meeting with Fred about Cunningham; he had a feeling it would be a difficult discussion.

He was thoroughly convinced that Cunningham was innocent. It seemed obvious that the scion of a family that had been dominating the region for nearly a hundred years would want nothing to do with Lincoln Savings or a man like Charles Keating. If nothing else, Cunningham was a patrician and a snob.

Bob found it easy to believe that Berkman gave assurances about where his money would be used, but then, when he faced a cost overrun at a different location, looked at the contract with Cunningham and realized he could move some money around. Or planned the contract that way, just in case. It was all logical.

To Bob.

Of course, that left a huge problem: Who the hell was the killer?

Bob was nearly done with his coffee when Marcus joined him. It was another beautiful morning; birds were singing and the air smelled sweet.

"We need to fence in the yard for Oscar," Marcus said.

"Mmm, yes. And lay in supplies. And find a vet. Alex said the pups go home at eight to twelve weeks. He said Sophie is a great mother and the pups all look healthy."

At 7:00 Bob showered and dressed, while Marcus went to his study where he tried to concentrate on the article he was supposed to be writing. He hadn't told Bob—he didn't want to worry him when he had a murder case on his mind—but he was beginning to wonder if UCSD was the right fit for him. All his colleagues seemed to want to talk about was the academic pecking order—who was up, who was down, who was a "lightweight," who was "deadwood." At his previous job, as a lowly assistant professor at Harvard, and in graduate school at Princeton, those conversations happened, but rarely. The talk was almost always about substance, whether it was someone's work, or a new book, or what was happening in the world.

Marcus was beginning to miss the Ivy League, which shocked him. Sure, it was snobbish and elitist and full of itself, but it was also a place where intellect mattered above all else. Here, he wasn't so sure.

He was lost in such thoughts when Bob came in and kissed him good-bye. "Sex when I get home."

"I guess that's what I have to expect when I marry a younger man."

"Damn right."

Bob arrived at the office a few minutes before the 9:00 o'clock meeting and quickly drank a cup of coffee. On his way to Fred's office, he ran into Duane, who looked nervous. They found Perez and Bobbitt and Chief Murphy already seated around the DA's conference table. Murphy began.

"Cunningham's fingerprints match the prints on the glass that was left on the credenza in Berkman's office. We didn't find them anywhere else in the office, including the prints on the broken glass on the floor. Those prints match no one in any of our systems. We're calling him Mr. X."

Fred exhaled loudly.

"What about Cunningham's alibi?" Duane asked.

Perez responded. "We have Ms. Hargrove coming in for an interview this afternoon at four. But she knows why we want to see her, and she already told us she was with Cunningham that afternoon and evening."

"Then," Fred said, "it's obvious he could have hired someone to do the murder. He had the means."

Murphy responded. "Of course that would leave a cash trail. So far, your accountants haven't found it."

"Look harder." Fred said, looking at Duane, who had removed his glasses yet again.

Murphy was undeterred. "I really don't think he's responsible for the murder."

"Why the fuck not?" Fred looked disgusted.

"Because his investment might have yet paid off. Because Cunningham's not an idiot. If he was going to kill Sam, he wouldn't have done it on the day he had an argument with him in his office. Unless he already had a killer waiting in the bushes, which is . . . It's just not logical."

Fred glanced at Duane, who had made similar arguments already.

"Then we're nowhere," Fred said.

Perez shifted his weight in his seat and then spoke. "We need more information about Berkman's personal life. His friends, social acquaintances. Maybe he was having an affair. We start by asking the mayor some questions tomorrow."

Fred made a face, but Perez continued. "If we need to, we try to get a judge to compel his shrink to discuss the content of his therapy. We might get lucky and find a sympathetic judge, although that's tough."

"Let's hold off on that for now. And be careful with Amy. She's not in great shape. I saw her over the weekend."

That surprised everyone in the room, but no one said so.

"Have the accountants go through Cunningham's finances dollar by dollar. What's the going rate for a hit like this these days?"

Perez answered. "Seventy-five to a hundred thousand."

"That's a lot of money," Murphy said. "Unless he kept that much cash in a safe somewhere, which would be stupid, especially if he's an investor, we'd find a trace."

Fred asked Duane to stay behind, and the meeting broke up.

39

In the hall, Perez told Bob the plans for the afternoon interview with Lucy Hargrove. After he left, Murphy pulled Bob aside. Bob smelled cheap men's cologne.

"Why is your boss so obsessed with Cunningham? He didn't do it."

Bob wasn't sure what to say. "I really don't know. I just got here. I know there's a lot of pressure, a lot of press. He's feeling the heat."

"We all are," Murphy responded. "The heat is part of the job. Reporters have been all over my office. But putting the wrong guy on trial would blow up in everyone's face, especially his. Just keep that in mind," he added as he left.

Back in his office, Bob sat down and closed his eyes. He wondered how, after just a few days, he was in the middle of a battle between the police chief and the DA over a high-profile murder.

Duane came in to tell Bob he would be in court on another case that afternoon. "You'll have to observe the interview with Lucy Hargrove by yourself," he said.

Bob told him about his exchange with Murphy.

"He's right, of course," Duane said. "Falsely accusing anybody, especially someone like Cunningham, would be a disaster in a case like this."

He paused and walked over to the window, where he stared out at the parking lot. "Check in with the accountants this morning, see if they've found anything else, and then take the rest of the day for bar prep. We're set to talk to the mayor tomorrow morning at ten . . . at her house. I'll meet you here and we can drive up together."

He left, and Bob walked down to talk to the accountants' office.

"Morning. Anything new?"

Adelman looked glad to see him. "Not much. But there is one thing."

Bob got his notebook out.

"It's from a few years back. As best we can make out, Berkman's cash flow was getting really tight, he was over-extended. In his business, there are a lot of estimates based on projections—how many units would sell, how fast, at what price, and so on. If the estimates are off, which could happen for many different reasons, cash could get tight. The profits from one project are needed for the next one. And so on."

Adelman retrieved a folder from a file cabinet.

"This happened around 1985 or '86, based on sluggish sales at a condo project in Orange County called Catalina Vista."

Bob waited.

"Slow sales, bad cash flow . . . and then suddenly there was an infusion of cash. Around a million."

"And?"

"And we don't know where it came from."

Bob thought for a moment. "A bank? A loan?"

"That's just it, there's no trace. Everywhere else, loans are carefully documented. There's a paper trail. This money seems to have fallen from the sky. There's no record of where it came from or of an equivalent amount being repaid."

"I see."

"Is that unusual?"

"In this kind of business, yes. It's the kind of thing that could trigger an IRS audit. Should have, really. But it didn't."

"So you think . . ."

"I don't know what to think, other than that Berkman was lucky. Or . . ."

"Or?"

Adelman hesitated and looked uncomfortable. ". . . Or had friends in high places."

Bob thought for a moment. He was about to stop asking questions, but then heard himself continue. "When was Amy first elected mayor?"

"1986."

"And before that?"

"She was on the County Board of Supervisors."

"Is it possible," Bob chose his words carefully, "that one of the Berkmans took the money from personal funds?"

"Well, Sam didn't. We have all his account records." The emphasis was on "his."

40

Bob went straight to Duane's office, where Cathy told him he was tied up, and probably would be all morning. He was about to go back to his office and read bar folders but then had an idea. He headed for the archives.

The archivist greeted him with a smile. "What can I do for you, young man?"

"I need to see everything you've got on Amy Berkman."

Philip nodded. "Well there's quite a lot." He walked to a file cabinet and pointed to a drawer. "Pretty much everything in there."

"Shit."

Philip smiled.

"Sorry."

"No need to apologize. Compared to the language one usually hears around here, that was practically Shakespeare."

Bob laughed and opened the cabinet. He also consulted various reference books on the shelves.

He worked through the clippings for the rest of the morning.

Amy Berkman, née Singer, was born into a middle-class family in Sherman Oaks, an LA suburb in the San Fernando Valley, where many Jewish families had settled before and after World War II. She had one brother, a dentist named Ira. Their father, who ran a small lumber and paint business, was Jewish. His immigrant parents had been brought to California as children from Poland and Lithuania.

Amy's mother was Protestant. In most respects a typical housewife of the era, her family was heavily involved in the Foursquare Church founded by Aimee Semple McPherson, the colorful and often controversial Pentecostal evangelist. McPherson, Bob knew, was the basis for the Jean Simmons character in *Elmer Gantry*. As an adult Amy called herself a Methodist but often said she had "great respect" for all faiths.

Amy herself was always a good and diligent student in the public schools as she grew up. She enrolled at UCLA as an undergraduate, where she worked part-time in a campus cafeteria.

After graduating, she briefly thought about becoming an actress, took acting classes and singing lessons, but then decided to apply to law school. She attended Boalt Hall, the Berkeley Law School, and after that moved to San Diego, where she quickly got a job working in the home office of a Republican member of Congress. She married Sam Berkman in 1976, soon after she turned 30, and successfully ran for the County Board of Supervisors right after her second child, Daniel, was born.

As a supervisor and then as mayor, Amy advocated the streamlining of local government and supported local conservation efforts. She pushed for tax reform and better funding for public schools. She was pro-choice and friendly to the LGBT community. Her biggest disappointment, she had admitted in a recent interview, was that she was not able to convince the powers that be in Washington that San Diego needed a new airport. The current one was severely hampered by a lack of space to expand, and its location caused serious noise problems in several San Diego residential neighborhoods, including Ocean Beach.

Bob had noticed the noise there; it could be deafening.

One set of articles in particular caught Bob's attention: Amy was very good at raising money for her political campaigns, mostly from the local business community, especially for her first run at mayor. One article described the campaign as "awash in cash." Another said she "had more money than she knows what to do with." She spent some of the cash on sophisticated television ads, relatively unusual for a mayoral race at the time.

The timing fit; Sam's windfall could conceivably have come from Amy's campaign cash. That would have violated various California laws, Bob assumed.

Around 12:30 Philip said he was going out to lunch and invited Bob to join him. They walked over to a small Greek restaurant near the office. Philip seemed to be a regular.

"So," Philip asked after they had ordered, "who did it?"

Bob laughed. "At this point, we have no idea."

"So I gather. Mr. Cunningham is innocent?"

"Looks that way."

Bob realized there were absolutely no secrets in the DA's office.

"I'm not surprised. I mean, I'm sure he looked down his very long nose at the Berkmans, but I can't imagine him risking everything. He's young, after all."

"Tell me," Bob asked, "what's your impression of Amy?"

"Well," Philip said as he dug into his salad, "she's someone to watch. In terms of the future, I mean. I'm sure she's aiming rather high."

"And would you say she's an honest politician?"

Philip seemed surprised by the question. "I couldn't say, really. I don't follow the ins and outs of local politics all that carefully. What I mostly know about her is that she's a moderate Republican, which is a dying breed, and that could limit her future. San Diego is quite laissez-faire when it comes to social issues, but the rest of the country. . . ." Philip didn't finish the thought.

Bob thought for a minute. "And do you have any impression of the marriage?"

"None whatever. I've never really understood straight folk."

Bob was startled; he hadn't really stopped to consider whether Philip was gay or straight. He felt a pang of guilt; like many people his age, he hardly thought about older people in terms of relationships, or sex. And then he felt glad to have an ally, or a potential ally, as well as a friend.

"Tell me about you," Bob said with a smile.

"Oh, well. Me. Nothing much to tell. Grew up in Chicago, went to school there. I'm a bookworm, always have been. I was the last person in America to get a television. Degree in library science. Landed here by accident, with someone, who promptly left me. So here I am with my clippings."

Bob laughed. "You'll have to come over one night and meet Marcus, my partner. He's from Chicago as well, and also a bookworm."

"Yes I heard. He's starting at UCSD, isn't he? I'd enjoy meeting him."

They paid their separate checks and walked back to the office. It was getting hot, and the crispness that usually hung in the air had disappeared. Bob wondered what was going on; it was disorienting.

"Santa Ana," Philip said. "The wind shifts and comes in from the desert. It can get hot and very dry; the humidity can go down to single digits. Raymond Chandler weather, his line about the wind making meek housewives look at knives and think about murdering their husbands. When it happens in winter, it's great, but in the summer it can be awful. And, I gather, the crime rate goes up."

Bob went through a few more clippings, grateful for the building's dark hallways and air conditioning. He thanked Philip for his help, and for their conversation over lunch, and returned to Duane's office.

41

Bob found Duane eating a ham sandwich at his desk, and offered to come back later.

"No, no, it's fine, come in."

"The accountants have turned up something else. Maybe significant, maybe not."

"Go on."

Bob filled him in on the sudden appearance of $1 million on Berkman's balance sheet, with no indication of where it came from. Duane put down his sandwich.

"Maybe he just took it out of personal funds."

"That's the thing, they have those records, and can't find any trace of it."

Duane frowned.

Bob hesitated. "And the thing is . . ."

"Yes . . . ?

"Maybe it's a total coincidence, but this happened when Amy was running for mayor. Her campaign had lots of cash, according to pretty much every news source I've looked at."

Duane sighed heavily. "I don't see how she could transfer that much money without setting off alarm bells all over the place. Not to mention putting her campaign in jeopardy. And maybe risking jail."

"If you say so. But . . ."

"But what?"

"I think we should ask her tomorrow if she knows where that money might have come from. Without accusing her of anything. Gauge her reaction."

Duane closed his eyes for a moment. "That will be a barrel of laughs. Is there anything else?"

Bob said no and went back to his office. He had about an hour before the scheduled interview. He stared at the binders, closed his eyes, and grabbed one at random. It turned out to be Civil Procedure in California. He dug in and did his best to stay awake.

At 3:30 he made his way to police headquarters. He found Perez at his desk and walked with him to the by now familiar two-way mirror outside the interview room. Bobbitt, Perez explained, had the day off.

Lucy Hargrove arrived at 4:00, alone. She was wearing a beautiful yellow silk dress, pearls, and high heels, the very picture, Bob thought, of a confident attorney. She sat across from Perez, who stood and shook her hand. If Bob had walked past her on the street, he would have guessed that she was a model. He couldn't shake the feeling that he had seen her somewhere before.

"Ms. Hargrove, you've said that on July 7th you spent the afternoon and evening with James Cunningham at his home in Carlsbad. Can you tell me what time you arrived and what time you left?"

Hargrove said she arrived around 3:30 and did not leave until 9:00 the next morning.

"And Mr. Cunningham was present during that entire time span?"

"Yes."

"You're absolutely sure?"

"Yes."

"Did Mr. Cunningham mention that he had just spoken to Sam Berkman?"

"He did not."

"And what was his demeanor?"

"No different than usual. He did not seem upset or distracted, if that's what you're asking."

"And what is the nature of your relationship with Mr. Cunningham?"

"We have sex."

Her candor seemed to take Perez aback, but he went on.

"And how long has this relationship been going on?"

"Not that it's any of your business, but on and off for about five years."

Perez did some quick calculation in his head.

"That means your relationship began while Mr. Cunningham was still married to Judith Powers."

"That is correct."

"Were you aware of the fact that Mr. Cunningham was married when your relationship began?"

"Yes. To answer the next question, yes, I do have some

idea of why James looked for sex outside his marriage."

"And?"

" The answer is that he and Ms. Powers did not enjoy the same kind of sex."

Perez did not miss a beat.

"And what kind of sex is that?"

Hargrove paused, for effect, Bob thought. As she might when questioning a witness in court.

"Intense."

"I see. Would you call your . . ."—Perez paused to find the right word—". . . sessions violent in any way?"

"I would call them intense. I suppose some others might say they bordered on the violent."

"I see."

"But you would not?"

"No."

"Are you ever afraid for your safety in these . . . sessions?"

"If I were, I wouldn't go back for more, would I?" Hargrove was clearly enjoying this.

"Has Mr. Cunningham at any time discussed with you his financial investment with Mr. Berkman?"

"He mentioned casually some time ago that he was making the investment, but he hasn't mentioned it since then."

After a few more perfunctory questions, Perez thanked her for coming in.

"Always a pleasure to help our boys in blue. Of course," she said, tossing her hair, "our police force wear khaki, though some of them do wear those very attractive shorts." She paused. "And you," she said looking Perez over from head to toe, "mostly wear dark polyester."

And with that, Lucy Hargrove smiled and took her leave.

Perez came out to join Bob.

"I feel," Perez said, "like I just made soft-core porn."

And then Bob suddenly remembered where he had seen Lucy Hargrove. As an undergraduate at Brown he had once been invited to a gay and lesbian party by someone he hardly knew. When he got there, there was a bisexual, soft-porn film playing on the VCR.

Lucy Hargrove was in it.

42

Back in his office, Bob looked up Lucy Hargrove in Martindale-Hubbell, a reference work that listed active attorneys. The dates fit.

He knew there were plenty of people who had no choice but to work themselves through school and chose to work as an escort or do porn, as a way of making a decent amount of money in a short amount of time. Or as a lark. He and Marcus had run across people like that before.

Maybe that's what Lucy was doing. He was sure she wouldn't have used her real name—no one in porn did—and that she believed the film was so obscure, it wouldn't come back to bite her.

So to speak.

But still, it was quite a surprise. It was a risky thing for a future attorney to do.

Of course, she might not have known at the time that she'd end up a lawyer.

He decided he wouldn't tell anyone what he had discovered, unless it somehow became relevant to the case. At the moment, he didn't think it was.

He was getting ready to leave the office when the phone rang; it was Jennifer.

"How's the prep going?"

"Not bad. When I have time to study. Not much of that these days."

Bob hadn't decided how to deal with Jennifer. He still felt the need to be careful around her, but hadn't had much time to think beyond that. Should he confront her? Avoid her? He wasn't sure.

He hated this kind of thing; it made him think of high school. Or junior high. Who said what to whom. Who was in, who was out.

Games.

"I was wondering if you'd like to meet for a quick coffee or drink."

Bob glanced at his watch. He did have a little time; it was just after 5:00.

"All right, sure. It will have to be quick. Where?"

Jennifer suggested Leo's, a new coffee and wine bar in Hillcrest.

It was a short drive. Outside the entrance, Bob came face to face with Sandy Nelson, the mayor's chief of staff. Bob smiled and said hello; Nelson grabbed Bob's arm and pulled him aside.

"Sandy, you'll have to excuse me, I'm meeting someone," Bob said, trying to sound nonchalant.

Nelson smiled and, after a moment, let go.

"Sorry, this will just take a moment." Nelson put his hands in his pockets. "The interview tomorrow with Amy. I assume you'll be there?"

Bob nodded.

"I'll be there as well. I just wanted to emphasize how

traumatic this has been for her. I hope you guys can understand that."

"Of course." That's an odd thing to say, Bob thought; of course they know her husband was just murdered.

"Are you getting anywhere on the case?" Nelson asked.

Bob took a moment to think about how to reply.

"Sandy, I can't really comment on an open investigation. You must know that."

"Sure. Well," Nelson fumbled for words, "see you tomorrow." He smiled stiffly.

Bob watched him walk to his car.

43

Jennifer was waiting for him at a table on the back patio, which was full of potted plants and ivy crawling up trellises. She ordered a glass of white wine; Bob chose an espresso: he wanted his wits about him.

"Listen," she said, "I have a confession to make."

"Oh?" Bob tried to sound nonchalant.

"After we talked about the Berkmans, Fred called me. He asked how your prep was going, and I told him it was going fine. I . . . thought it was odd that the District Attorney took the time to contact me."

"Yes," Bob said, trying to keep his voice as neutral as possible, "it does seem odd."

"I mean, he's got a lot going on. A new ADA prepping for the bar is routine."

"Right."

"Well, then he asked me if I knew what you were thinking

about the Berkman case. I was really surprised. Shocked, actually. But, I mean, he's the DA, he's in charge. I thought he must have his reasons, and he is my employer."

"True." Bob hadn't thought of it that way.

"So I told him about our conversation. That you had asked about the Berkmans' marriage."

"I see."

"The whole thing made me uncomfortable. Extremely uncomfortable. But he caught me by surprise. I didn't have time to think it through." She paused. "And I hope I didn't land you in hot water."

Jennifer looked at him, expecting him to respond; when he didn't, she shifted in her chair, swallowed, and went on.

"I don't know what's going on, and really, I don't want to know. But I felt awkward about the whole thing. I probably shouldn't have said anything. But it was just so out of nowhere. And I'm sorry if I made a mess for you."

"Well, I appreciate your telling me."

And he did. But he didn't want to discuss it any further. He could believe Jennifer was taken by surprise and didn't know what to say when Fred called. What he couldn't really believe, and what made him both anxious and a bit angry, was why the DA was keeping such close tabs on him.

It just didn't make sense. It was Duane who was his direct supervisor. Fred was the DA in a huge office in a large city with dozens of active cases. Why was he doing this?

For a few more minutes they talked in a desultory way about the bar exam, and then Bob said he needed to be getting home. They agreed to stay in touch.

Marcus was listening to Joni Mitchell and making a mess in the kitchen. Bob kissed the back of his neck and stared around at all the pots and pans and bowls.

"Um, what is that?"

"I don't know. It may resemble lasagna when it comes out of the oven."

Bob laughed. "I'll make a salad just in case. So we don't starve."

44

The next morning he dressed carefully for the interview with the mayor, which, he hoped, would be a turning point in the case. If anyone could supply information that might lead to a killer, it would be Amy.

He met Duane as arranged and they set out for La Jolla. Bob took notes in the car as they went over what questions needed to be asked. He also decided to ask one of his own. In for a penny, in for a pound.

"What's your impression of the Berkman marriage?"

"Hard to say," Duane said. "I only saw them at events—fundraisers, receptions, that sort of thing. Fred knew them personally. He hasn't given any indication that the marriage was troubled, or headed for divorce court, and the cops haven't found anything, but who knows what really goes on in a marriage. I mean, I had a case where a wife shot her husband in cold blood and everyone who knew them was shocked, including their teenage kids."

Bob pondered that. What would people say about his relationship with Marcus? He knew some gay men would say they were selling out to "straight" values and couldn't possibly be happy. A friend of his from college had told him as much.

"You're insane," the friend had said. "In a couple of years you'll be bored and depressed and feel like you're missing out."

But they were happy. And Bob didn't think he was missing out on anything . . . except, maybe, when Marcus cooked.

The Berkman house was high on the western slope of Mount Soledad, about a mile and a half from the shore, with a commanding, if distant, view of the ocean. The lawn and shrubs were immaculate; the driveway was full.

"That's Fred's car," Duane said, pointing to a late-model Toyota.

"Did you know he would be here?" Bob asked, alarmed.

"No."

A young boy riding a tricycle near the front door smiled up at them.

"You must be Daniel," Duane said, smiling.

Daniel nodded vigorously.

"Well it's nice to meet you, Daniel. My name is Duane and this is Bob."

"Okay," Daniel said and pedaled away. Bob stared at him for a moment.

They rang the doorbell. An assistant wearing black slacks and a white shirt showed them in.

"The mayor will be with you shortly," she said, before striding away along the green marble floor of the foyer.

A curved staircase led up to a second floor. On the left was a rather grand dining room, and to the right, a tastefully decorated living room. Perez and Bobbitt nodded them in.

Bob glanced around the room. A few abstract art prints on the walls, several books, beige furniture, and what looked like hand-hooked, Santa Fe-style rugs covering floors of polished wood. The room had a high, sloping ceiling.

After a few minutes they heard voices, and Amy Berkman walked in with Fred at her side. Sandy Nelson, the mayor's chief of staff, came behind them. Amy and Fred were both smiling. They looked comfortable together. Quite comfortable, Bob thought.

The mayor was an attractive woman of indeterminate age, with a round face and black hair tightly pulled back. Her skin was flawless. She was wearing dark gray slacks and a silk blouse in the same color, low heels, and pearl earrings.

That does not look like a woman who just lost her husband to murder, Bob thought to himself. Of course, she was a politician, and she knew how to present herself as calm and collected.

"Gentlemen," she said by way of greeting.

Fred introduced everyone, and the mayor shook everyone's hands.

"I'm going to leave you all to it," Fred said. "I was just here to make introductions."

Amy smiled again, touched his arm for a fraction of a second, said, "Thank you for coming," and then she turned to the four men.

"There's coffee in the dining room," Amy said. "Why don't we go in there." It was an instruction, not a question, Bob noticed. Clearly the mayor was taking charge.

The dining table seated eight. A side table held a tall silver urn, china cups, and a plate of pastries.

"Please, help yourself."

As he poured himself coffee, Bob noticed the series of photographs arrayed at the back edge of the side table, including one showing Amy with Maude Strauss Cunningham at some sort of gala. Both were in long gowns and had broad smiles on their faces.

Amy took a seat at the foot of the table, where Sandy Nelson had already placed her cup, and everyone sat down. Nelson sat to her left.

Duane spoke first.

"Thank you for seeing us. And may I say, for all of us, how sorry we are for your loss. We're doing everything we can to find out who did this, and why."

"Thank you," Amy said simply. Her expression changed and became serious, as if she just now remembered that her husband had been murdered.

"We'd like to start," Perez said, "with the day it happened. We understand Mr. Berkman arrived at his office after lunch. Do you know what he did that morning?"

"Yes. As I was leaving the house, Jeffrey Kahn arrived. He and Sam were golf partners and often played a quick round first thing in the morning. I assumed that was what they were planning to do."

"I see. We've interviewed your maid, who said that in fact they did not leave the house for some time. Any idea why?"

Amy seemed genuinely surprised. "I'm not sure. I suppose they got to talking. They were good friends. Or perhaps Sam's knee was acting up. It's been hurting on and off, and when it's bad, he doesn't play."

"Had he said anything to you about his knee?"

"No. Not that I can remember."

"Can you tell us, had Mr. Berkman—"

"Please, you can call him Sam."

"Thank you. Had Sam been upset about anything? Worried? Was anything beyond the usual on his mind?"

"Well he was juggling various business problems, but that was routine, really. He didn't seem especially upset about any of them, no."

"Did you know he was scheduled to see James Cunningham that day?"

"No."

"Did you know Mr. Cunningham well?"

"Not well, but we did know him. We saw him at various events. He was also a contributor to my campaigns. I believe he was here at the house for a dinner at one point."

"Did you know he was heavily invested in one of Sam's building projects?"

"I knew he was invested. I didn't know the details, or the extent."

Amy sipped from her coffee cup.

Perez nodded to Duane, as if to say, you take it from here.

"Were you aware of anyone who was angry at Sam, or fighting with him?" Duane asked.

"No, not at all. That's one of the reasons this is so shocking. As far as I was aware, everything in his business was humming along nicely."

Bob noticed she mentioned the business. Of course, that left out his personal life. Their personal life.

"So you weren't aware of any difficulties at a development in Oceanside?"

Amy paused for a moment, seeming to choose her words carefully. "I knew there were some cost overruns, but I didn't know the details."

Duane went on.

"Were you aware that Sam had placed three million dollars in a Swiss bank account?"

Bob watched her carefully. For just a fraction of a second, Amy looked shocked. And then it was as if a mask descended over her face, the mask of the competent mayor and loving wife. Nelson shifted in his seat.

"Yes, I was. He was thinking of investing in some European property, I believe."

"Do you know the details of that?"

"No, sorry, I don't."

"Our accountants have been through Sam's files, and there's another transaction we're unable to follow."

"Oh?"

"Yes, it's from 1985-86. There's a deposit of $1 million into Sam's business account, and we can't find the source of those funds."

Amy sipped her coffee before answering.

"I have no idea. I really did not get into the weeds with Sam over his business. And that was years ago."

Bob noticed her tone had become rather cool. With a glance at Duane he said, "There was a bequest in Sam's will to a Gerald Otley in New York. Do you know Mr. Otley?"

Amy's expression was blank. "No. I assume he was an old friend of Sam's."

"Do you know how they met?"

"Sorry, I don't."

Perez resumed questioning.

"I'm sorry to get personal, but we need to ask this. Were you aware Sam was seeing a therapist?"

Amy looked down. Nelson shifted again.

"Yes, I was."

"And do you know why he was?"

"My guess would be unresolved issues from earlier in his life."

"And do you know what those were? Did you discuss it?"

Amy looked perturbed. "Those are private matters."

Duane spoke up. "Amy, we have to ask. As I'm sure you can understand, nothing is private in a murder investigation."

"I can tell you I'm sure it had no relation to his murder. The therapy started months ago. I'm really not prepared to say more."

"All right, that's your prerogative at this point. But that may mean we have no choice but to compel his therapist to violate confidentiality."

Amy made a gesture with her hands, as if to say, do what you have to do.

Perez spoke next.

"Would you say your marriage was on solid ground?"

Sandy Nelson clenched his jaw. Amy simply stared at Perez, and there was controlled anger in her voice. She answered very slowly.

"Yes, Detective. Our marriage was on very solid ground."

Duane took over again, as if to smooth out the tension once more. "Is there anything Sam did or said in the weeks leading up to his murder that might help us find the person who did this?"

"Believe me, Duane," Amy said, turning toward him, modulating her tone, "I've asked myself that question a dozen times. There's nothing. Everything seemed normal. Of course, I'm very busy. He's busy. When we're together—when we *were* together . . ." she said, trailing off as her voice quavered, though Bob wondered if the emotional tremor was real or a convenient choice. She was, after all, a master politician. ". . . Sam and I tried to spend as much time with the children as possible. Our time together was focused on them."

"Of course." Duane paused, as if to give Amy time to recover her composure. Then, businesslike, he asked, "Can you give us the names of Sam's closest friends? It might help if we speak to them."

"Yes, I expected you to ask that." Amy got up and

retrieved a sheet of paper and handed it to Duane.

"Thank you, Amy. And thank you for seeing us. If you think of anything that might help us, please let me know."

"Of course." She stood, as composed and polite as her normal self, and walked them through the foyer to the front door. Nelson slipped ahead and opened it for them, clearly eager to see them gone.

Duane hung back and quietly spoke a few words to Amy. Bob tried, but couldn't hear what he said, though he noticed Amy smiling as Duane came out to join him.

As they got in their cars, Perez reminded them that they would meet in Chief Murphy's office at 2:00. Duane started his engine, and Bob took one more look at Daniel riding his tricycle along the sidewalk.

45

As Duane pulled out of the driveway, Bob looked back at the house. Neither of them said anything for a couple of minutes. Then Bob spoke.

"I don't think she knew about the $3 million in Switzerland."

"Really?" Duane sounded surprised.

"For a fraction of a second she looked surprised. I think she made up the idea of European property on the spot. The accountants haven't said there was any trace of such a thing."

"Maybe it was a new idea, hadn't gone very far."

"I suppose that's possible. But I don't think she knew. Which says to me we have to learn more about the therapy. And the marriage."

Duane let out a breath.

"And," Bob went on, "why was Fred there? Seems very odd. And they seemed very cozy together."

"They've known each other a while."

"I think it was more than that."

"What are you suggesting?"

"I don't know."

"Don't let your imagination run away with you. It's important in this job to stick to the known facts."

"Well, one known fact is that the DA wasn't supposed to be there this morning, and was. It's beyond odd that he didn't tell you he was coming. And another fact is that he and the mayor seemed awfully cozy."

"Are you always this suspicious?"

"Isn't that an asset in this job?"

Duane smiled. "I suppose."

They were silent until they returned to the office. Bob didn't see Duane again until they all met in Chief Murphy's office at 2:00. Before that, he checked with the accountants, who said there was no mention at all of a European property deal, but that they would keep their eyes open.

Bob ate another tuna sandwich at his desk, then went to the archives. He asked Philip to see if he could find any clippings about compelling testimony from a psychiatrist.

Just before 2:00 he and Duane drove to police headquarters. Perez and the chief were waiting for them.

"Perez has filled me in on the basics. What were your impressions? I want to hear from both of you."

Bob wondered what Perez may have said, but Duane spoke first.

"Well, she wouldn't really talk about Sam's therapy, so if we want to know what was going on, we would have to get a court order for the therapist. She denies that there was any trouble in the marriage. All in all, not terribly useful. There is one interesting fact about the morning of the murder. Amy thought Sam was going to play golf, but the maid told us he and his friend stayed in the house. We need to talk to the guy right away. We also got names of other friends."

Murphy nodded, and turned to Bob.

"What about you? Can you add anything?"

"Well, these are only my impressions. But I did not think she knew about the money in Switzerland, even though she claimed she did. There's no trace in Sam's accounts or files of any plans for European property."

Perez said, "I agree. I think she was lying about that."

"Which means," Murphy said, "we have to wonder if she was lying about anything else."

"And . . ." Bob hesitated.

"And?" Murphy asked.

"And I don't understand what Fred Stevens was doing there. He hadn't told Duane he would be there, which I think is odd. And . . ."

"Yes?" Murphy leaned forward.

"And it was only a moment when they walked in, but I thought Fred and Amy were very cozy with each other."

Murphy stroked his chin for a moment. "Duane, why was your boss there?"

Duane looked extremely uncomfortable. "He said he was there to make introductions. They do know each other pretty well."

"I want you to ask him why he was there. If you don't want to, we will."

"No, no. I'll ask him."

Perez spoke again. "I agree, they were pretty friendly, considering her husband had just died."

"Okay," Murphy said, getting up. "We need to dig deeper into the Swiss account. We need to talk to the psychiatrist again. And we need to interview the golf buddy and the others ASAP."

Everyone nodded, and the meeting broke up.

While Duane went to the men's room Perez pulled Bob to the side.

"I don't know what your boss is up to. The big boss, Fred. I don't really trust him in this situation. Keep your eyes and ears open."

The two attorneys were silent as they drove back to the DA's office. Just as they reached their building, Bob spoke up.

"When the Chief of Police asks me a direct question about a murder investigation, I have to answer truthfully," he said. "I hope you agree."

Duane still looked unhappy and uncomfortable. Bob added, "Or at least understand."

"Yes, of course," Duane said irritably.

Bob was sure he didn't mean it.

46

The next morning, a Wednesday, Duane called Bob at home at 7:30 as he and Marcus were having breakfast. He told him Perez had scheduled an interview with Sam's golf buddy, Jeffrey Kahn, at 11:00 o'clock at his home in Mission Hills, and another interview with Marcia Aaron, Sam's psychiatrist, for 4:00 that afternoon.

When he got off the phone, Bob sighed heavily.

"I'll bet Perry Mason never sighed like that," Marcus said, trying to cheer him up.

"Perry Mason was a defense attorney. I play for the other side. And Perry always won. We don't even have a good suspect."

"Well," Marcus said, pouring more coffee into both their cups, "you can always quit and do corporate law. Get rich and support me. We could buy a big house on the ocean."

"Don't tempt me."

As he reached his office the archivist slipped in behind him. "I could only find a few clippings about cases in which psychiatrists were compelled to offer testimony," Philip said, handing handed him a file.

"Thanks. I owe you a lunch," he said as he began to read through the articles. There were three cases, but in all three, the doctor's client was the suspect, alive, and the DA was able to argue that the client likely was a danger to others. That didn't fit the facts here at all.

Bob read through his bar prep binders until it was time to interview Kahn. Cathy gave him the address and told him Duane was out of the office and would meet him and the others there.

Kahn's house was a tidy two-story bungalow at the end of a cul-de-sac. Bobbitt, Perez, and the two lawyers all arrived at the same time and approached the front door together. It was painted cobalt blue.

The moment Kahn opened the door, Bob's gaydar went off. The man's gym-toned body, his clothes, his cologne, even something about his self-conscious manner, all unmistakably broadcast a clear message. The décor of the house and the books on the coffee table in the living room cemented the impression; there was no doubt in Bob's mind that Sam Berkman's golfing partner was gay.

They settled in the living room. Kahn offered coffee, which they all declined. Perez asked him about the morning Sam was killed. Kahn's story matched the mayor's; they were scheduled to play golf, but Sam's knee was acting up, so they didn't.

"What did you do instead?"

"Oh, you know, we drank coffee and talked. And we spent some time with Daniel. Cindy wasn't there, she was at day camp."

Cindy was the Berkman's daughter.

"Do you recall the conversation?"

"Not really. The news, the weather. It was very casual."

"And what time did you leave?"

"Around eleven. Maybe elevein-fifteen. I had a client to see."

Kahn was an architect. In background research they had learned that he had designed the Berkmans' house.

"Do you know of anyone who might have wanted to harm Sam?"

"No. I wish I could help you, but I can't think of anyone."

"Did he seem upset or worried about anything in particular? More than usual?"

"No, not at all."

Duane then spoke up, reluctantly, Bob thought.

"As far as you were aware, were Sam and Amy having any difficulties?"

"Well," Kahn said, after a moment, "I don't think being married to a politician is easy. I mean, Amy was hardly ever around. The kids were young. Are young. The press is always hovering. But they managed. I thought they managed well, all things considered."

Perez thanked him for his time, and handed him a card, asking him, as usual, to be in touch if he thought of anything else that might be relevant.

The four men walked to their cars.

"Nothing," Perez said, clearly frustrated.

"Although," Bob said, "it's the first hint we've had that the marriage wasn't perfect."

"What marriage is?" Perez replied.

"Um, listen," Duane said hesitantly. "I talked to Fred this morning and asked him why he was at the house yesterday."

"And?" Perez asked.

"He says Amy invited him over at the last minute, wanted a preview of what was coming, who would be there. He didn't think he could say no." Duane paused. "They're friends. They've known each other a long time."

"Okay, I'll tell the chief."

Bob waited to see if anyone said anything about Kahn's sexuality, but they all seemed oblivious. Or thought it didn't matter. He wondered if he should say something but didn't have time to think it through before they got in their cars and left.

47

The afternoon interview with Sam's psychiatrist was tense and unproductive. Dr. Aaron was adamant about protecting her client's confidentiality. She didn't budge when Duane tried to persuade her that they truly needed her help to find Sam's killer. Perez threatened to obtain a court order, though Duane and Fred agreed with Bob that they would get nowhere asking a judge to compel her to reveal a patient's secrets.

Over the next ten days, they interviewed many of Sam's friends; nothing helpful emerged. No one thought the marriage was in trouble, or that Sam was under extra stress. None of them could think of anyone who could have done it. Everyone had an alibi.

The accountants could not discover any additional information about Sam's Swiss bank account. The San Francisco police finally got back to them about Sam's funeral: there no one suspicious there, or nearby, that day.

Bob wrestled with the question of whether to talk to Duane and Perez about his belief that Jeffrey Kahn was gay, but he couldn't come up with a reason to do so. After all, lots of straight people have gay friends. Kahn and Sam met when Kahn designed the house; they started playing golf together; they became friends. Made sense.

The gay movement was busy debating whether sexual orientation was a totally irrelevant trait, like eye color or being left-handed, or whether LGBT folk were fundamentally different from others; queer, in a word that was gaining popularity in some circles. The irrelevancy argument was far more useful when it came to questions of legal reform, and that was what Bob cared about—his civil rights, and Marcus's, and everyone else's. He tended to see being gay as an irrelevant trait. Marcus knew some academic colleagues who were busy getting invested in something called queer theory, and Bob was interested in their intellectual arguments, which could be dazzling, but both of them thought of their own sexual orientation as something that really didn't matter, when all was said and done.

Irrelevant.

Bob said nothing about Kahn. Sam had a gay friend; not an issue.

Meanwhile, everyone involved in the investigation was frustrated and irritated with the lack of progress. One morning a headline read "Police Stumped."

In between interviews, Bob did his best to concentrate on his bar exam prep.

Finally, though, his travel to New York to interview Gerald Otley was approved; he arranged to leave on a Saturday morning, spend the weekend with his parents in Connecticut, and then interview Otley on Monday.

48

The night before he left they joined Bob's brother and his wife for the ACLU fundraiser. It was billed as an event for "drinks and dessert," and Alex had bought two $100 tickets for Bob and Marcus, calling it a welcoming gift. Over a quick light supper beforehand, Carol filled them in about Sophie, her puppies, and Jay, who was thrilled to have more dogs to play with. Bob demurred when Alex asked how the case was going; the truth was, he thought to himself, it was going nowhere.

They ate in Del Mar, a well-to-do suburb just north of La Jolla, home of a famous race track once frequented by movie stars. Bob loved hearing the Hollywood gossip, even if it was twenty years old. Lucille Ball and Desi Arnaz would rent a place in Del Mar every summer, Carol told them, where they would spend the morning at the beach and the afternoon at the track. Bing Crosby was a regular, as was FBI Director J.

Edgar Hoover with his live-in "companion," Clyde Tolson. Bob noticed that even Marcus, who affected disinterest, was listening to Carol's every word. He smiled.

The fundraiser was held at a sprawling estate in Rancho Santa Fe, farther to the north and slightly inland. There was valet parking and a huge crowd, both inside the mansion and on the terrace and the extensive lawns, which led to an inviting pool and tennis courts. The hosts were Roberta and Orren Maxwell; Orren was a screenwriter; as far as Bob could tell, Roberta was simply a California rich man's wife. Waiters in white jackets circulated with trays of champagne and nibbles, and tables set with china, linen napkins, and an unending supply of sterling silver, held an array of desserts, including flaming cherries jubilee.

Alex immediately started greeting and glad-handing people, leaving Carol with Bob and Marcus.

"Oh, my," Marcus said as he surveyed the scene. "The A-list."

Carol laughed. "Yes. Potential donors."

Bob was surprised. "So Alex is serious about going into politics?" Up until now, Bob had thought it was all abstract, not really a concrete ambition.

"Yes," Carol sighed. "He is. It will mean a lot more evenings like this. You have no idea how that thrills me," she said sardonically.

"Does he realize what he's getting into? I mean, the constant fundraising, it would drive me crazy."

Carol gave a resigned shrug. "It seems to be something he really wants."

Alex turned back to them and motioned for Carol to join him next to an important-looking man.

"Duty calls," she said.

Bob watched her join Alex. As she walked toward him, she carefully composed her face into a smile; when she reached him, she put her hand on his arm and cast him an adoring look that reminded him of Nancy Reagan.

Bob looked at Marcus and they both shuddered.

He saw that Duane was there, and they smiled at each other. After a few moments Duane joined them and introduced his wife, Elizabeth, a very attractive blonde who reminded Bob of Grace Kelly. They all chatted until Duane saw someone he needed to see and excused himself.

"I hope this case isn't too hard on you," Elizabeth said. "I know it's a tough one."

Bob nodded. "It is. But I'm learning a lot."

Marcus excused himself to say hello to an academic colleague. Bob found Elizabeth charming and friendly. She enjoyed chatting about their three children, their schools, even how a picturebook life "can have all the normal problems and surprises . . . if you let reality in," she said, smiling with a sideways glance at their hostess.

Across the lawn, Marcus finished his conversation with his colleague and turned to look for Bob . . . and came face to face with Caroline Peters.

49

He was astounded. Peters had been caught up in the investigation of the death of one of Marcus's students at Harvard—a young man who had been sharing a house with Bob before he was killed. Caroline had been engaged to the victim's brother; Marcus had been drawn into the investigation by his parents.

"Why, hello there," Peters said. "What are you doing in our little ol' neck of the woods?"

Marcus had little doubt Peters was very tipsy, if not drunk. He explained that he and his partner had just moved to the area, that he'd be teaching at UCSD.

"And you?" he asked. He knew she was a Californian by birth, from a fabulously wealthy family, rather like the Cunninghams—though from San Francisco, if he remembered correctly.

She told him that she now lived in Rancho Santa Fe.

He steered her toward Bob. "Caroline, this is my partner, Bob Abramson."

She drained her glass. "Yes, I remember. You were at Trip's memorial service." She shook Bob's hand.

"And what do you do, Mr. Abramson?" she asked as she took another glass of champagne from a waiter.

"I've just gone to work for the District Attorney."

"You work for Fred? How interesting. Are you folks getting anywhere on the Berkman murder?"

"Well, the investigation is ongoing."

"Yes, I'm sure it is. Amy is a friend of mine." Peters took another long drink. "Have you met her?"

"Yes, we interviewed her."

"And did she tell you," Peters asked, pausing for effect, "that she was fucking your boss?"

"I beg your pardon?" Bob said. Both he and Marcus froze.

"Amy and Fred have been carrying on for years. Everyone knows. Well, not everyone."

She laughed. Peters was clearly enjoying herself.

Bob didn't know what to say. He just smiled back.

A handsome man in a tight-fitting, Italian suit walked up

to Peters and took her arm.

"Have a good evening, gentlemen," she said, as the Italian suit led her away.

Marcus was holding a glass. Bob took it out of his hand and took a long gulp.

And he realized why he had stared at young Daniel Berkman on his tricycle the day they interviewed the mayor. He looked like Fred Stevens.

50

Bob and Marcus found Alex and Carol and told them they had to leave. Alex told Bob to be sure to give their parents his love that weekend.

"Look," Marcus said in the car, "she was drunk. I'm not her favorite person—that investigation in Boston. Maybe she's making it up."

"Maybe. But something tells me . . ."

"If it's true . . ."

"If it's true, the whole case could be compromised. If a lot of people know the mayor and the DA were carrying on . . ." Bob didn't finish his sentence.

His thoughts were racing. Could Daniel really be Fred's son, or was he imagining it? Did Sam know about Amy's affair? Is that why he was planning to leave? Was that why he was in therapy, and why there was money in a Swiss bank account?

It would all make some sense.

How much did Duane know about Fred and Amy?

Did Amy's affair somehow lead to Sam's murder?

And then the next logical question: Did Amy arrange for Sam to be murdered so she could be with Fred?

It was all too much. Bob felt sick to his stomach. He wanted to go to sleep and hide under the covers. But he had to get up the next morning and fly to New York.

"Pooh, you need to talk to Duane about all this. You can't hide it."

"Right. But first I'll talk it all over with Dad. He'll know how to handle something like this. I hope."

He slept very little. After breakfast Marcus drove him to the airport.

"Give my love to Mom and Dad," Marcus said as he hugged Bob at the airport curb. "And try not to worry."

Bob always felt happy when Marcus called his parents Mom and Dad. They had spent a good deal of time with them in Connecticut, and Marcus was very fond of them. He had been amazed at how comfortable they were with their son being gay and bringing home a man older by ten years, as if it were the most natural thing in the world. Bob's parents introduced Marcus to their neighbors and friends, and even their rabbi, as their son-in-law.

Although Marcus didn't talk about his family much at all, and wasn't close to them, one night he had explained to the Abramsons that his own family was light years behind. They didn't disapprove, exactly, but they made it clear they had no interest whatsoever in hearing about Marcus's personal life.

Bob napped fitfully on the plane, but as much as he tried not to think about the case, he kept wondering about what they had heard from Caroline. His gut told him it was probably true. He remembered seeing Fred and Amy together at her house that morning, and all the times Fred encouraged the investigation to go easy on her.

He got to JFK on time, took a cab to Grand Central where he caught the train, and finally arrived in Danbury around 10:00 p.m.

His parents greeted him with hugs at the front door.

"My God," you look awful," his mother said. "What's going on?"

"You have no idea."

"Come into the kitchen. Eat something."

Bob smiled. Every Jewish mother's solution to every problem.

They peppered him with questions, and he talked about Marcus and the house and what it was like to live in San Diego. He told them about seeing Alex and Carol and about the puppies as he ate two slices of poppyseed cake and drank iced tea.

"Okay, so what's bothering you?" Bob's dad finally asked.

"Is everything okay with Marcus?" his mother asked anxiously.

"Oh God, yes. It's not that." His mother looked relieved.

"It's this case they have me on." He turned toward his father. "Tomorrow I need to talk it through with you."

"Sure. Of course. Get a good night's sleep. It will help clear your head."

51

Given his jet lag, Bob didn't get to sleep until close to 2:00 a.m., and he didn't wake up until 10:00. He slept well; as he always did at home. He smiled as he remembered the first time he brought Marcus here to meet his parents.

After a shower he found them in the garden drinking coffee.

"There's lox and bagels."

Bob made himself a plate, poured himself a cup of his mother's strong coffee, and joined them.

"Tell us more about the house," his mother said.

He told them as he ate: the colors, the yard, what they were planning for the garden. And about the puppy to come.

"We were thinking," his dad said, "we might fly out over the holidays. Maybe between Christmas and New Year's. Enjoy a little sun. See Marcus, Alex, Carol, Jay."

"That would be great," Bob said, and meant it. He missed being close to his parents. It was the one thing he truly regretted about moving to the West coast.

After breakfast Bob's mother excused herself to meet a friend for tennis. She added, "You can discuss everything with your father while I'm gone."

His father said he needed to make one phone call, and then they could talk.

Bob closed his eyes and tried not to think. He could smell his mother's roses. He drank more coffee. After a half hour or so, his father came out and said he was ready.

"We better do this inside," Bob said.

They settled in the den, and Bob narrated the whole story from beginning to end. This could be a summation for a jury, Bob thought to himself, and it's a pretty good one.

His father only occasionally interrupted to ask a question. Bob tried to be careful to separate what was known from what was an assumption, or conjecture, or not proven.

"Well, that's the story. So far," Bob said finally. He sipped more coffee.

"Jesus Christ. It's like something out of a Hollywood

potboiler with Lana Turner."

"Well," Bob said, "it is California, after all."

"Okay, so some things are pretty obvious. You have to talk to Duane about what you've heard. Maybe he knows about the affair; maybe it's not true."

"Yes."

"And the DA needs to recuse himself from the case. Even if he's not having an affair with the mayor, he apparently has a personal interest in seeing her move on and then running for her job. He can't be involved. It could blow up in his face, in everyone's face."

"That's gonna be tough."

"You may have to get the police chief involved. He'll see the conflict right away. Maybe he already has. Or the detective—Perez? He already asked you to keep an eye on the DA."

"Okay. I can talk to Perez, and maybe Chief Murphy. Or Duane can."

"Forget about the paternity issue. That really is a private matter. And there's no way to prove it. This new technology—DNA—is too new and controversial. Concentrate on whether Sam was planning to leave the marriage, not on the intimate reasons, and whether the mayor could have possibly been involved in his murder."

"Oy."

"I know. But there's no way to avoid the question. Maybe she wasn't. As you say, she's clearly not dumb. But look for a cash trail. Talk to her security detail. You'll have to convince the police to look into it."

Bob nodded.

"What a case to get involved in right off the bat. I'm sorry."

Bob tried to smile.

"Look at it this way," his dad said. "Everything that comes after this will be easy."

52

Bob relaxed and enjoyed the rest of the weekend with his parents—his mother's cooking, his old room, going out on Saturday night to their favorite Italian restaurant where they ran into a few neighbors.

But Bob noticed, with some delight, that he missed Marcus, even though he would be away for only a couple of days. He called him on Sunday.

"So what have you been doing?" he asked.

"Oh, you know, the usual. Cavorting with local pornstars."

"Well, that's a relief. I was worried you might get bored without me."

Marcus got serious. "Did you talk things over with Dad?"

"Yes, very helpful."

"Good. When will you be home? I have to tell the boys when to leave."

"I see a witness Monday morning, then catch the plane. The plane is supposed to land at five California time."

"Okay, I'll make sure they're all gone by then. And, hey, I'll cook us something for dinner."

Bob winced. "They'll probably feed us on the plane."

"And it will be awful. I'll make something. I promise not to let anything explode in the oven."

Bob laughed and then said quietly before hanging up, "You know what? I do love you, you know. Even your cooking. See you tomorrow night."

The next morning after breakfast his father dropped him off to catch the 9:00 o'clock train for Manhattan. As usual, his mother stuffed a bag of homemade brownies in his case as he was saying good-bye.

He was scheduled to meet Gerald Otley at his job in Soho; he took the subway and arrived a few minutes early. He stopped for a take-out coffee and looked in some gallery windows. It was a lovely summer day, but Bob noticed that he missed the feel of the ocean in the air he usually felt in San Diego.

The art gallery was in a cast-iron building on the first floor, with what looked like expensive apartments above it.

Otley was an athletic, young-looking man of around 35, expensively dressed and wearing a Rolex. The gallery was empty. The paintings being displayed, Bob thought, were awful attempts at Abstract Expressionism. They shook hands, and Otley showed Bob to a seating area with comfortable leather chairs at the rear of the large, rectangular room.

"I see you already have coffee. So, what can I do for you?"

Bob explained that he worked for the San Diego district attorney and was part of the team investigating Sam Berkman's murder.

"What a horrible thing. It made the news here, you know. That's where I first learned about it. I hope you catch whoever did it. Sam was a very decent man."

"We're wondering how you knew each other. In Mr. Berkman's will, all the beneficiaries are identified as friends or relatives. In your case, there's only a name."

Otley took a long drink of what looked like mineral water from a crystal glass.

"We met about three years ago. I'm afraid I don't remember the exact date."

"Can you be more specific about the circumstances?"

"Well, I assume you know about my sordid past." Otley let out a short, self-conscious laugh.

"Yes. You worked as an escort." Bob kept his tone neutral and, he hoped, friendly.

"Yes. For a relatively brief time. I was broke, New York is expensive . . ."

"I understand. I'm not here to judge. Did Sam hire you?"

"Yes. He had gotten my name from a friend. I don't know who."

"I'm sorry to pry, but this is a murder investigation. What can you tell me about your encounter?"

"Well, that's the odd thing. It wasn't really an 'encounter.' Not in the usual sense. I went to his hotel—the Waldorf—assuming Sam wanted sex of some kind. But we ended up just talking. I know that may be hard to believe, but I would swear to it under oath. Or take a lie detector test, or whatever you need."

Bob was surprised, and paused for a moment. "And what did you talk about?"

"In my work, I had gotten quite good at reading people. My sense of Sam was that he was interested in having sex with a man, but had never done it. Or if he had ever done it, only rarely."

"I see."

"He was confused. He talked about his family. He clearly loved his wife, but I got the sense that he felt neglected. I think he was one of those men who marry because they think it's the right thing to do, never having really explored what they really wanted."

"And that was it? You just talked?"

"Yes. For about two hours. He seemed relieved to have

finally had a chance to talk about his situation."

"And was that your only encounter?"

"We exchanged letters a few times. It started with a letter from Sam thanking me for the talk."

"Did you save any of those letters?"

"No, sorry, I didn't."

Bob knew the next questions could produce important information, so he chose his words carefully.

"Did Sam's letters give you any sense that he and his wife were moving toward divorce? Or that Sam was moving toward coming out as gay, or bisexual?"

Otley took another sip and thought for a moment. "If you had read between the lines, you might have formed that impression. But there was nothing explicit, no."

Bob wrote down Otley's answer word for word, which took a moment.

"Is there anything else you can tell me about Sam? Did he ever mention an enemy, or a dispute with someone?"

"No, nothing like that. We exchanged just two or three letters. Then there was radio silence. Then after a long while, I don't remember quite how long, I got another letter from Sam saying he had gone into therapy to try to figure things out, and that he hoped to see me the next time he was in New York."

"I see."

"I'm afraid I didn't respond. By then I had had some trouble with the law and had given up that life. I never heard from him again. If he tried to call the number he had, that phone had been disconnected."

"So you might say that the bequest was to thank you for being a friend?"

"Yes, I assume so. It shocked me."

Bob thought the story sounded plausible, although, of course, there was no way to check it. He thanked Otley for his time and for speaking frankly, and asked him to call if he remembered anything else.

"Sorry I didn't save those letters. I hope you catch the bastard, whoever he is. How long are you in town?"

"I leave for the airport straight away."

"Ah. Well, enjoy San Diego. I know it's beautiful. Try Black's Beach."

Black's Beach, Bob knew, was a nude beach near the UCSD campus.

53

On the plane home, Bob avoided the lunch American Airlines was serving in coach and ate his mother's brownies instead, saving the last one for Marcus. He thought about what Otley had told him.

Was it believable? If Sam Berkman was confused about his sexuality, or if he was gay but, because he was married, had so far never acted on his impulses—and Bob knew there were many such men—it could explain his being in therapy, and his therapist's reluctance to talk. And it would easily explain his wife's turning to Fred Stevens for a sexual relationship.

But this was all conjecture, Bob thought. And it doesn't really help find the killer.

Or does it? Maybe Sam had begun to act on his impulses. A lot of married men hire escorts. Maybe the encounter in the office before the murder was a local tryst with an escort that went awry. They still hadn't identified the fingerprints on the broken glass on the floor.

Or maybe Sam turned to drugs out of sexual frustration. Some people did. Maybe the murder was a local drug deal gone wrong. But the police would have picked up some hint of a drug habit by now, wouldn't they?

And what about the $3 million in Switzerland? How did that fit in? Was Sam planning to escape the marriage?

Assumptions, theories, conjecture. Unanswered questions. This case refuses to come together, Bob thought. A piece is missing. But what? He closed his eyes and dozed.

When he opened his eyes again the captain was telling people they were passing over the Grand Canyon. Bob looked out the window at the spectacular view..

By 5:30, having retrieved his luggage, Bob was heading home, the cab's window open so he could enjoy the ocean crispness in the air. Marcus hugged him at the door.

"You just missed the last pornstar."

"Not if it was the guy who got in the cab when I got out. I hope he didn't completely ruin your appetite."

"Take a shower. Dinner's almost ready."

When Bob joined Marcus on the patio for baked chicken and rice and salad, he said, "Not bad! You've been practicing."

He woke up at 5:30 the next morning, still on Connecticut time, and took a cup of coffee out onto the patio. He tried to work out how he could implement his father's strategy of asking the DA to step back from the case. He couldn't possibly confront Fred by himself. Duane could, though Bob sensed that he would be reluctant to do that.

The police. They could do it. They could, first, check out Caroline's claim that Fred and Amy were involved. Then they could say that they were worried that the DA's involvement could compromise the case in one way or another.

Yes, that might work. Fred would probably still hate him for bringing it up, but maybe not enough to fire him. After all, he didn't go snooping around for the information; Caroline Peters was drunk and blurted it out.

Maybe it wasn't even true.

But, as his father pointed out, even if Fred didn't have a personal interest in protecting the mayor, he had a professional interest in not damaging her politically if he secretly, or not-so-secretly, hoped to succeed her.

Stevens needed to step back, whether he liked it or not.

Then Bob remembered Cathy.

He went to his desk and looked for the card she had given him with her home phone number. He found it, waited until 7:30—Cathy had young kids, she'd be up—and called her at home. He asked her if she would set up a meeting with Duane, Perez, and Murphy to go over what he had learned in New York and "other things."

She told him that Duane would be in court all morning, but she'd arrange for them to meet over lunch or early in the afternoon.

He spent the morning digging into his bar exam binders. The meeting would be at 12:30 over sandwiches, Cathy had told him.

"Tuna, again?" she had asked.

"Oh, let's go wild," Bob had said. "Make it turkey."

54

Duane, Murphy, and Perez were already in the library when he arrived, carrying a legal pad with his plan of attack—new information to share, ethical concerns, and his request—all laid out in advance. My first trial court strategy, he told himself.

"So, kid," Perez said, "what's up?"

Bob took a swig from his ginger ale.

"Two developments in the last couple of days."

"Two?" Duane asked.

"Yes. The first came out of nowhere."

He narrated the story of what Caroline Peters had said at the ACLU fundraiser as straight-forwardly as he could.

"Of course," Bob said toward the end, "she had had a great deal to drink. The champagne was flowing freely. But clearly we have to check this out."

Bob looked around the table. All three of them looked uncomfortable.

Finally Duane spoke.

"It's true. We don't have to check it out."

Bob, Murphy, and Perez stared at him. Duane took off his glasses.

"Fred and Amy have been involved. I don't know when it started exactly, but it's been going on for a while. And it may have cooled off lately. But it's true."

"Do you realize," Murphy said, in a voice that would terrify anyone, "that both you and Fred have withheld vital evidence in a murder investigation?"

Duane said nothing. He looked down.

Bob then added what he had been told by his fellow ADA Billy Louis—that Fred wanted to run for mayor.

"That's no great surprise," Perez said.

This time it was Bob who was shocked.

"Look, guys, I'm new to this, obviously," Bob said, "but if Fred has at least a professional interest in protecting Amy, so he can move up the totem pole, I don't see how he can be involved in the case in any way."

"You're right," Chief Murphy said. "We didn't know about the affair. But on the political front, we were waiting to see if there was any evidence pointing to Amy as a suspect. So far there isn't. But with this new information, we will need to dig deeper. And Fred has to stay out of it."

Everyone nodded, and Murphy continued.

"Duane, you and I will talk to Fred. Today."

Duane nodded again.

"And then there's Otley," Bob said. He told them everything about the interview.

They were all silent for a minute.

"Well," Perez finally said. "If Sam was . . . confused, that could explain why Amy had an affair."

"And," Murphy added, "it does look like maybe he was moving toward divorce, putting that money in Switzerland." He paused, then looked directly at the ADA. "Now here's what we're going to do, Duane. You and I are going to talk to Fred. He's going to step back."

Duane grimace and almost visibly shrank in his chair; then he composed himself. To Bob it seemed his boss was relieved at being forced to do the right thing.

Murphy continued. "Perez, you and your partner need to interview Miss Peters, sober this time, I hope, and then all of you—and Bobbitt, too—are going back to Amy. It's time she told us the truth. We're going to talk to her friends, and we'll continue talking to Sam's friends. And if any of this hits the press I don't give a damn. We've been jerked around enough. More than enough."

Everyone nodded.

"And," Murphy again looked at Duane, "you and I are

going to have a heart-to-heart, right now."

Bob and Perez got up to go.

In the hallway, Perez said, "good work, kid. But if I were you, I might start scanning job ads."

55

When he got back to his office, Bob realized he hadn't touched his turkey sandwich; he was about to go back to the library for it, but stopped himself; Duane and Murphy were probably still at it. Sitting back down at his desk he tried to gauge how much hot water he would be in.

They couldn't out and out fire me, he half-thought, half-hoped. They'd have to know he'd be likely to go public, guaranteeing that Fred's affair with Amy would end up on the front page. He'd be tempted to do that, he realized, even if it did hurt his career.

So they wouldn't fire him. But they could, and would, make him miserable in various ways. That was the real danger.

Two years. He would need to stick it out for two years. That, he knew, was the minimum length of time needed to look respectable in a job such as this. Then he could move on. By then, if he was lucky, he'd have marketable trial experience.

He was hungry; if his boss was still being chewed out by the police chief at this point, too bad. He headed down to the library just as the two came out into the hall. Duane was red-faced again.

"I'm glad we caught you," Murphy said. "We're about to go talk to Fred. I've made it clear to Duane, and I will make it clear to Fred, that if they retaliate against you in any way whatever for bringing this information forward, there will be hell to pay. If either one of them so much as looks at you funny, I want to hear about it immediately."

Bob had no idea what to say, or think. "Okay. Thank you," was all he could manage.

They disappeared toward Fred's office. Bob took his sandwich back to his desk, took a bite, and put it down. It was soggy and unappetizing.

It was all feeling like too much. He'd barely arrived here, and already the Chief of Police was protecting him from his superiors. How did this all happen?

He realized that once again he needed his father's advice, and he quickly dialed the office in Connecticut. Just punching in the numbers made him feel better. Unfortunately, Jacob was in conference, according to his secretary Bev, whom Bob had known since junior high school.

Bev took down his phone numbers and then asked, "How's it going out there in the land of the lotus-eaters?"

"Oh, you know. Blue skies, palm trees, the Pacific Ocean. What could go wrong?"

"Well, that sounds ideal. I'll have your dad call you as soon as he gets back."

Bob had been reviewing his study binders for more than an hour when Duane knocked, opened the door, came in without an invitation, and sat facing Bob's desk.

"Look," he said, "I'm sorry. Truly sorry. To have put you in this position. Murphy laid down the law with Fred, and with me. Fred is going to step back from the case, informally for now. No briefings, no information."

"Okay, good."

"For what it's worth, which may not be a lot, he

doesn't think Sam was considering divorce. But he's not sure. What he is sure about is that Amy did not want to split up, and would have fought it. For the kids, if for no other reason."

If Amy was going to bring the kids into this, Bob realized, he needed to say something, despite his father's advice. He made another split-second decision.

"About the kids," Bob said.

"Yes?"

"When we were there and we ran into Daniel in front of the house, I noticed something unusual about him—about his face—that I couldn't quite figure out."

"And?"

"And, after hearing from Caroline Peters, it seemed . . . possible."

"What seemed possible?" Duane looked genuinely puzzled.

"That Daniel's real father is Fred, not Sam."

Duane turned pale. "Oh, Jesus."

"Sorry, but if Amy is going to bring the kids into what she is and is not willing to do, then obviously that's a relevant piece of information. If it's true."

"There's no way to know. We can't ask her."

"Why not?"

"We just can't."

Bob gave him a look. "Then ask Fred."

"He would go straight to her. And why does it matter?"

"You just had a conversation with Chief Murphy! *Nothing* is to be held back, Duane. I mean, imagine that Amy knows Daniel is Fred's son. They've been carrying on an affair. For whatever reason, the marriage to Sam has gone cold. She wants him out of the picture."

"Are you saying she had someone murder her husband?"

"I'm saying it's possible. Isn't it? I mean, it wouldn't be the first time a wife wanted her husband dead."

"God," Duane said. "I feel sick."

Neither of them spoke for a long minute.

"Okay," Duane said. "We'll ask for Amy's personal bank records. I've been over this with Murphy. If she doesn't offer them voluntarily, we'll get a subpoena. She'll know we could go that route and then it would hit the press, so she'll almost certainly agree. We'll interview members of her staff and security detail. If there's any evidence at all pointing to her, we'll confront her about Daniel. Otherwise, no. It's a private matter."

Bob nodded reluctantly.

"Murphy's on the way to Amy's office now to ask for access to bank accounts. He'll set a time for another interview. Meanwhile, the detectives are setting up meetings with friends, relatives, associates . . . anyone close to her. Murphy's assigning additional detectives. You sit in on the most important ones."

"Okay."

"And Perez is trying to set something up with Caroline Peters for tomorrow."

Duane started to leave, then turned back. "One thing we need to know—how exactly do you know her?"

Bob explained about Marcus and the sordid murder of his former student, and Caroline's relation to the family.

"Wow."

"Yeah."

"The Howard family? Even I've heard of them. Aren't they, like, at the top of the social ladder in Boston?"

Bob inhaled.

"Not anymore."

56

Bob's father returned his call just as Marcus and Bob were finishing a Chinese take-out dinner. Bob filled him in.

"That police chief sounds like he has his head screwed on right. Thank God."

"Yeah, but, I mean, short of threats, the DA could still make my life miserable."

"Well, that's true. It's possible. Maybe even likely. So you keep notes. Of everything. Everything you do, everything they say. Everything. At home. Not on a computer. If there's a pattern of mistreatment, even minor, talk to the chief."

"Okay."

"My guess is that they'll pretty much leave you alone. They're not going to risk any kind of scandal, which you would have the power to create, even just based on what you know so far. So you pass the bar, keep your head down as much as you can. If you have to leave before two years, you leave. You'll be able to explain what happened."

"I guess so. But I can't believe things are so complicated so fast. It's insane."

"It's criminal law. I hate to say I told you so . . ."

"I know, I know. Dirty hands. But I thought the dirt might take a little longer to get here." Bob paused. "I know it's late there. Give Mom my love. Tell her I'm okay. Even though I'm not."

Marcus had cleared the table while listening carefully to Bob's side of the conversation. "So," he said, "let me get this straight. Your boss's boss, the district attorney, is having an affair with the mayor."

"Yes."

"And you think he may be the father of one of her kids."

"Possibly."

"And now the chief of police is protecting you from the DA."

"Uh-huh. At least, I hope so."

"This sounds like a bad Hollywood miniseries."

Bob laughed. "That's what my dad said when I was there. Actually, he thought it was a Lana Turner melodrama. You've downgraded me to television."

"Well, I'll say this much, your job certainly is interesting."

The phone rang. As he picked up the receiver, Bob said, "And unending." A moment later he mouthed, "Duane."

When he got off the phone, Marcus looked up from the sink, where he was finishing the dishes.

"Well?"

"Well, we interview your friend Ms. Peters tomorrow at 10 o'clock," Bob said. "At her house in Rancho Santa Fe. I'm just so eager to see her again."

"Lucky you."

Bob smiled sardonically as he looked at Marcus, barefoot and wearing shorts and a T-shirt.

"Get dressed, we're going out," Bob said on an impulse.

"Out? Where?"

"A movie." Bob grabbed the local newspaper and looked for movie times, then looked at his watch.

"We can make a show at the Ken."

The art-house theatre in Kensington was showing the just-released *Sex, Lies, and Videotape*, about a Louisiana lawyer sleeping with his wife's sister. All Bob could think about throughout the film was Fred and Amy.

"That was not the movie I needed to see tonight," Bob mumbled as the lights came up.

57

The house in Rancho Santa Fe was in an even grander part of town than where the ACLU fundraiser had taken place. The estates were larger and the terrain was hilly. Beautiful. Peaceful. Where the super-rich would hang out.

Bob found Perez and Bobbitt sitting in their car outside the Peters estate a few minutes before 10:00. As soon as Duane pulled up, Perez reached through his window and rang the buzzer outside the gate. He waved at the security camera as well, and the gate opened to a long drive.

The house had an enormous fountain in front of it and an oval drive paved in limestone. It was built in a French provincial style, which was, Bob thought, ridiculous in Southern California, where the influences were Spanish, not French. Typical of the rich, Bob thought, to create whatever environment they like.

A maid in uniform admitted them and showed them through the foyer, where they caught glimpses of room after room filled with antiques and, no doubt, priceless art, including what looked like a van Gogh. She showed them to an enormous terrace overlooking a swimming pool. In the distance were what looked like stables. A second maid came out with four coffee cups on a silver tray.

"Ms. Peters will be down momentarily."

The men took their cups and sipped their coffee. After a few minutes, Caroline came out from the house with a man trailing behind her. She was dressed in a riding costume, slacks tight around the ankle, red jacket, and high leather boots, which gave her a menacing air—which, Bob had no doubt, was her intention. In the daylight, Bob could see that she had aged considerably since the first time he'd seen her, four years before.

She walked up to Bob and shook his hand.

"Mr. Abramson, would you introduce your colleagues?"

Bob did, and Caroline nodded to each.

Pointing to her companion, Caroline said "This is Joel Davis, my attorney."

"I know the Assistant District Attorney, of course," he said, turning to Duane. "So, what can we do for you?"

"Ms. Peters, when you ran into Bob at the recent fundraiser, you told him that Mayor Berkman and District Attorney Stevens were involved in a . . . relationship."

"I did."

"Can you tell us how you came by this information?"

Caroline smiled. "Amy's a friend, and she has confided in me."

"And do you know when the affair began?"

"No, not precisely, I only moved here about three years ago, down from the Bay Area. It was certainly in full . . . bloom by the time I arrived."

"Did you know the mayor before moving here?"

"Oh, yes. For years. We met a long time ago in San Francisco. At a fundraiser, I believe."

Perez took over. "Would you say the affair is still going strong?"

"As far as I know. I'm really not sure."

"Do you know if Sam Berkman was aware of the affair?"

"Well, since it was Sam's behavior that led to the affair,

I assume he did know, or at least suspect. In fact, Amy said as much."

"And what behavior would that be?"

Caroline took a sip from her coffee. "Sam stopped having sex with his wife."

Duane swallowed hard and resumed the questioning. "Do you have any idea why?"

"Well, I'm just guessing, but I think it would have something to do with Sam's own"—she paused and pretended to search for the right phrase—"sexual proclivities."

"Meaning?"

"Amy came to believe Sam played for both teams."

"By which you mean . . ."

"Do I need to spell it out? Very well. Amy believed Sam was bisexual. That he liked men."

There was silence while everyone took a sip of coffee. Caroline Peters looked satisfied at the men's discomfort.

Bob plunged ahead. "Has Mayor Berkman ever revealed anything about the paternity of her children?"

Caroline looked surprised for the first time that morning.

"My, but you have suspicious minds. No, Amy has not discussed that with me."

"Was she thinking about divorce?" Duane asked. "Or did she think Sam was thinking about it?"

"Amy did not want a divorce, I know that much. I don't really know about Sam. It wouldn't surprise me. But I don't know. I don't think they were spending much time together."

"Do you have any idea who might have killed Sam?"

"No, I don't. I do know Amy was very upset by his death. Really upset. I saw her the day after, spent several hours with her. A doctor came, she needed to be sedated."

"Can you think of anything else we should know?"

"Well," Caroline paused, "I know that Amy is nervous that the public might find out about the affair with Fred. And I know she has no interest in breaking up Fred's marriage. Fred and his wife are Catholic, and apparently the wife is devout. So I'm sure Amy would appreciate your discretion."

She seemed unaware, or unconcerned, that it was her own indiscretion that had tipped Bob off in the first place.

Bobbitt spoke up for the first time.

"It may not be possible to keep it quiet."

Duane and Perez glared at him.

"I would caution you to be careful," the attorney said, uncrossing his legs. "You could be getting into very murky legal territory here."

"We will do our best," Duane said. "But this is a murder investigation. We will go wherever we need to go."

Caroline stood up.

"Now, if you'll excuse me gentlemen," Caroline said, "I have a date with a horse."

Everyone stood.

"Oh, and Bob, say hello to Marcus for me. And ask him if he's ruined anyone else's life lately." She turned and disappeared.

58

Out on the driveway, the four men paused. "Now that," Bobbitt said, "is what I call a piece of work."

Everyone ignored him.

"Okay," Perez said, looking at Bob. "The information

you got in New York seems to be confirmed. We have to dig deeper into his personal life. The killer may be there."

Duane nodded.

"And there's no way to avoid talking to the mayor again."

Duane looked exasperated but again nodded.

"We've already begun interviewing her security team. The extra men the chief gave us have started on that. We're getting fingerprints. There's still Mr. X, the prints on the glass on the floor in Sam's office. That's our closest link right now to the perp."

Perez moved toward his car.

"I'll report to the chief about today and get back to you."

Everyone got in their cars and drove off. The front gate magically opened to let them pass.

On the drive back downtown, Bob thought about Sam and the struggles he must have been going through.

Coming out was never easy under the best of circumstances, Bob knew; it was always a struggle, even now, twenty years after Stonewall. And most people don't enjoy the best of circumstances. He knew many men hid their feelings from the world, their families, and from themselves, until sooner or later they could no longer ignore them.

He felt for Sam. He knew what it was like to feel something in yourself that you try to ignore but can't. A flaw, most people think at first. A problem. A quirk. A phase.

A fault line.

It will go away, you think.

If you're lucky, as Bob was with his parents, that feeling of fault doesn't last very long. But Bob knew that in some cases it can lead to long, slow agony that can express itself in all sorts of destructive ways.

It can crush you.

And it must have been especially hard with a wife and children. If Sam was a decent man at all, he would not have wanted to hurt them. So his particular struggle must have been intense. He was glad Sam had had at least a little bit of therapy. He hoped Dr. Aaron knew what she was doing; not every therapist was comfortable with issues of gay sexuality, even now.

Then Bob started to think about how the investigation could look into Sam's personal life beyond his marriage. One thing seemed obvious: Since he had contact with Otley in New York, he might have had contact with gay escorts in California.

And Bob realized with a sinking feeling that he might be the best person to guide that part of the investigation.

But how to manage it? There were dozens, hundreds, of gay escorts all over Southern California; they advertised in what Marcus called the gay rags, the gay press. There were two gay weekly publications in San Diego alone, as well as several in Los Angeles, and undoubtedly many more in San Francisco. Altogether there could be thousands of gay escorts in California; the police couldn't interview them all, no matter how many detectives got assigned to the case.

But, Bob knew, there were apparently a couple of "agents" who placed higher-tier escorts, mostly men coming from the gay porn industry. They advertised openly. Ben's Buddies even placed ads in the San Diego papers.

They could start there. Or they could look for guys who looked like Otley; maybe Sam had a type. Lots of men did.

Then there were the bars. And there was the list of Sam's friends the mayor had provided.

Bob sighed. Too much. How in the world were they going to follow all these possibilities? Even with extra detectives, the task looked gargantuan.

And what if Sam's murder had nothing to do with his sexuality?

What about the mayor? Her behavior after Sam was killed, as Caroline reported it, could have been a performance—that's what politicians did. Politics was theater.

Or she could have felt genuine remorse for having ordered or arranged the murder.

It was a quagmire. Quicksand. As Bob drove past Mission Bay on his way downtown, he wondered if he was drowning.

59

Bob spent the rest of the day trying to study for the bar exam, but found it difficult to concentrate. Everything was swirling in his head, Sam, Caroline, Gerald Otley, the mayor and her young son. He kept flashing on the murder scene and the autopsy.

At 4:00 o'clock Perez called and told him there would be a meeting in Chief Murphy's office at 5:30. Bob wondered why he wasn't hearing this from Duane or Cathy, but he said he'd be there. He called Marcus to tell him he'd be home a little late.

When he got to Murphy's office, Perez was there, but there was no sign of Duane or Bobbitt. Instead, Murphy introduced him to a detective—this one with blond hair who could have passed for a 1950s teen idol. Tab Hunter, maybe.

"Bob, this is Jason Thompson. He's been assigned to the case. I want the two of you to investigate Sam's personal life."

Bob had never seen eyes so blue. It wasn't normal for the police chief to decide what he would be doing—he didn't work for the police, after all—but everything was happening so fast he didn't see how he could object. Besides . . . Tab Hunter. He nodded his agreement.

"I'll inform Duane," the chief continued. "We'll all meet tomorrow at noon to see where we are."

Bob made a note on his calendar. I guess, he thought to himself, now that Fred and Duane are compromised, the police are taking control.

"At the moment," Chief Murphy said, "we have only one suspect, Cunningham, and there's not much implicating him. I suppose it's possible the mayor ordered or arranged the murder, but there's no evidence for that. You guys need to dig into the life Sam was keeping hidden. When someone lives that way, the perp is often found there."

"Right," Thompson said. "That broken glass. Those prints. We have to find that guy."

Perez led Bob and Thompson to an adjoining office and shut the door. "Jason is the first openly gay detective on our squad," he explained.

Thompson flashed a million-dollar smile.

"Together, we need the two of you to do what you can to explore that side of Sam's private life."

"Okay." Bob couldn't think of what else to say.

"I was thinking," Thompson said, "we could grab dinner and make some plans. If you're free."

"Um," Bob said, not realizing exactly what he was saying, "my partner is expecting me at home. But why don't you join us, we can talk there."

"Sure. Thanks."

Bob gave him the address. On his way to his car, he

stopped at a pay phone in the lobby and called Marcus.

"Pumpkin, I'm bringing home another pornstar. For dinner . . . No, he's not the dinner, he's the guest. And a member of the San Diego Police Department. Do we have any food?"

60

Bob drove home quickly and told Marcus what was happening. Luckily, Marcus had a casserole in the oven, enough for three.

When Thompson arrived Bob introduced Marcus, who turned around and silently mouthed "Oh, my God."

Thompson had loosened his tie and stopped for a bottle of wine. He and Bob went to the patio while Marcus figured out what to serve as a side dish.

"Nice place. You guys just move in?"

Bob told him the outlines of their story, meeting in a previous murder investigation in Boston, law school, moving to San Diego, buying the house with a UCSD mortgage.

"And you? What's it like to be a gay cop?"

"Well," Jason chuckled, "it was tough at first. But little by little the brass realized that having a queer cop could help in certain cases. Like this one. So it got easier. Especially after I made detective."

"Well, that's what progress looks like, I guess."

"Yeah. Step by step." He sipped his wine. "Tell me what you know about Sam. I got the broad outlines from Perez."

Bob filled him in, told him about Otley, gave him his impressions of the mayor and Cunningham.

"Do you think Cunningham is good for this?"

"No." He explained his thinking.

"And the mayor?"

Bob didn't know what to say. He chose his words carefully.

"I don't know. My gut says no, but I don't know. I don't think she'd jeopardize her political career. And I think the marriage was more of an arrangement at this point, for both of them. And maybe it was working for both of them."

Over dinner Jason told them his own story. He grew up in San Diego, the son of two elementary school teachers, an only child. He went to Cal State LA, majoring in psychology, and always wanted to be a cop. He was single.

"You guys are lucky, to have found each other," he said, surprising both of them.

"It's hard to believe someone like you would have trouble dating," Marcus said.

"Oh, I have plenty of dates," Jason said, laughing. "But most everyone I meet around here is pretty shallow. Body by Nautilus, brain by Mattel."

Marcus laughed, but Bob was surprised. He never thought a man who looked like Jason Thompson couldn't have exactly whatever personal life he wanted.

"We should talk about the case," Jason said. "I've got some ideas."

Marcus knew that was his cue; as he started clearing the table Bob and Jason moved into the living room.

"I think we do a few things off the bat," Jason said. "Talk to the escort agents. Some bartenders. I've never seen Sam around town, and I've already begun asking a few people. No one recognizes his picture, at least not yet."

"I'd guess," Bob said, "if he did anything in San Diego, he was super discreet. And given his relationship with Otley, escorts are probably the best lead. But we can't interview every escort in Southern California."

"No. But maybe a few. And the agents, definitely. And some of the A-list gays around town. I know a few. We can start there."

"And," Bob said, "we have to be careful about publicity. If we start asking too many questions in bars, and the story gets out that Sam was . . . whatever he was, there could be hell to pay."

"Yeah, well, it's a murder. Apparently first degree. The case may get messy. There's no way around that, no matter how careful we try to be."

Marcus brought out coffee. Jason declined, saying he'd be at the noon meeting the next day, and Bob and Marcus saw him out.

As they closed the door behind him, Bob said, "Why does everyone in this town look like they just stepped out of a Hollywood movie?"

Marcus hugged him from behind. "Pooh, what did you expect? This is California. It ain't the Ivy League. No more tweed."

Bob gripped his arms. "And you love me even though I'm not blond?"

61

Bob spent the morning with his bar prep binders and then joined Duane, Murphy, Perez, and Thompson in the conference room.

"Okay," Duane said, "where are we?"

"These two," Murphy said, pointing to Jason and Bob, "will look into Sam's personal life. We've been interviewing the mayor's security people and taking fingerprints. So far no match to Mr. X. The mayor agreed to turn over her bank records and financial statements; you need to get your money guy to go through them."

Duane nodded.

"Cunningham's ex-wife has resurfaced. We speak to her tomorrow. And we interview the mayor the next day. At HQ, not at her house."

The ADA looked surprised.

"The press," Murphy went on, "is already picking up that we're investigating the mayor. There's no way we can continue to protect her. She's going to have to take her lumps. We can say it's routine to look into a marriage in a situation like this, which is true, and that the mayor herself is not a suspect, which is also true, at the moment. We can try to keep her relationship with Fred out of it. For now."

Duane reluctantly nodded. Bob thought for the first time he detected an air of defeat on his face, as if his doctor had just given him bad news.

Murphy turned to Thompson.

"How are you going to approach the gay angle here?"

"Sam had that relationship with that escort in New York," Jason said. "He would have been discreet here in San Diego. I doubt he went to bars, but we'll make a few quiet inquiries. We're more likely to get somewhere with the escort angle, and maybe by talking to his friends."

"I agree," Bob said. "That's most likely where Sam went, if he did anything at all here in town."

"Okay, good," Murphy said. "Keep me informed."

When the meeting broke up Jason followed Bob to his

office. Jason said they were scheduled to meet with Ben of the escort agency that afternoon in Laguna Beach. They would need to leave at 3:00; Jason said he'd pick Bob up in front of the building.

"This morning I showed Sam's pictures to a few bar owners and managers," Jason went on. "Nothing. I told them to keep this confidential, but who knows. I think a press shitstorm is coming."

"Probably no way to avoid it," Bob said.

"What are those?" Jason asked, pointing to the binders.

"Oh, bar exam prep. I haven't taken it yet."

"I really enjoyed dinner last night," Jason said. "Marcus is older than you are, isn't he?"

Bob smiled. "Yes. Ten years."

"He seems like a great guy."

"He is."

"You guys are right for each other. I have a nose for that sort of thing. See you later."

Bob stared after him as he left. *We are right for each other*, Bob repeated silently. He smiled to himself. He had always thought that, almost from the moment he met Marcus. But he wondered how it showed.

At 3:00 he stood in front of his building. Jason drove up in a vintage baby-blue Thunderbird convertible, top down.

"I should have guessed you'd be driving a car like this."

"Why?" Jason looked genuinely puzzled.

"Because so far everyone and everything in San Diego looks like it came off a movie set."

"Well this," Jason said, touching the dashboard, "came second-hand from a little old lady in El Cajon. It was in bad shape, but I restored it."

El Cajon was a mostly working-class suburb east of San

Diego. Tab Hunter would play a mechanic who fell for a rich Debbie Reynolds, Bob thought. The car ran smoothly, and Bob couldn't help but notice Jason's biceps as he shifted gears; he was wearing a short-sleeved polo shirt and had put his jacket on the back seat.

I have to remember to buy polo shirts, he reminded himself.

Once they were out of city traffic, Jason asked Bob if he'd always wanted to be a lawyer.

"Well, kinda. I mean, my dad is, and so is my older brother. I guess it runs in the family."

"Do you think you'll stay with the DA, or move on? I know a lot of ADAs move on."

"I'm not sure. I mean, I just got here, and already the politics of my first case are driving me crazy. Who knows how this will end."

"That's the thing about homicide," Jason said, "it takes everyone places they usually don't want to go."

"I'm learning that fast. Maybe tax law, nice and quiet. Numbers, not corpses."

Jason laughed. "Nah, you'd get bored. Then you'll be unhappy and Marcus would leave you. We can't have that."

Bob smiled. It still struck him as amazing that Jason envied his relationship with Marcus, but there it was. And then Bob wondered if he was shallow himself for thinking a person's looks determined what his life would be like.

They drove in comfortable silence until they passed Camp Pendleton.

"Ah, Pendleton," Jason said. "Home of the sexually confused Marine. But they are cute, I'll say that much."

"Uh-huh. And I'll bet," Bob said, smiling, "you've known a few."

62

The address for the meeting with Ben turned out to be a small condo in a large complex near the commercial center of Laguna Beach, halfway between San Diego and Los Angeles. It was an ugly white stucco building, three stories high, that couldn't have been more than ten years old but already looked dilapidated and out of place, since most of the town was upscale and manicured.

They took the elevator to the top floor and knocked on the front door. It was opened by a young man wearing the skimpiest gym shorts and T-shirt Bob had ever seen.

They were ushered into a living room that contained two desks, a few chairs, and little else. It overlooked a parking lot in back of the building, and it was obvious no one lived there. The young man disappeared into another room. Sitting at one of the desks was an older man dressed in a flowered shirt talking on the phone. He had two gold chains around his neck and a large gold watch.

"Saturday, then," he said, hanging up the phone and standing up. He weighed a great deal more than was healthy for a man of his height and age.

"Gentlemen, please, take a seat. I'm Ben."

Jason and Bob pulled up two chairs .

"Can I offer you something to drink?"

Jason looked at Bob and then said "no thanks."

"So what can I do for the San Diego police?"

"We're looking into the murder of Sam Berkman, Mayor Berkman's husband. We have reason to believe he might have used your services. We'd like to find out if that's true, and who among your employees he might have met."

Jason slid him a photo of Sam.

"I should add," Jason said, "that we're not here to disrupt your enterprise in any way. We're only interested in this murder."

Ben smiled, lit a cigarette, and looked at the photo.

"Sorry, gents, but he does not look familiar."

"Does the name ring any bell?"

"No, not at all. Darren?"

The almost nude youth came in from the other room.

"Honey, does this man look familiar? Does the name Sam Berkman mean anything to you?"

Darren stared at the photo for a long time.

"I've seen him, maybe. At the Boom."

"How recently? More than once?"

"Mmm, a few times, maybe. Last time was maybe a few months ago."

"Do you recall if he met anyone, or left with anyone?" Jason asked.

"Sorry, no, I wasn't paying attention to him. He's not my type." Darren gazed at Jason as if to say, "You are, though."

Ignoring the flirtation, Jason continued, "What time of day would this have been?"

Darren thought for a moment. "Late afternoons, maybe."

"I see." Jason said. "Could you do this for us?" Jason went on, turning to Ben. "Could you show the photo to a few of your employees, see if anyone recognizes him? Especially anyone who might have gone down to San Diego, or who frequents the bar?"

"I can do that," Ben said. "Always happy to cooperate."

"Please," Bob spoke for the first time, "please ask anyone you ask about this to keep this confidential."

Ben chucked. "Well, I can do that, but I can't control them. Really, they're independent contractors. So to speak."

"Yes, we understand," Bob replied. "But whatever you can do."

Jason handed his cards to both Ben and Darren. "If you think of anything else, please get in touch."

"Sure, sure," Ben said.

Darren nodded and smiled up at Jason, who smiled back, cooly but politely. "Thanks for your time."

"By the way," Ben said to Jason as he stood up, "if you ever need to make some extra cash, give me a call."

Jason turned bright red, and he and Bob left as quickly as possible.

63

When they reached the parking lot, Bob asked, "What's the Boom?"

Jason looked at him incredulously. "The Boom Boom Room," he said. "A gay bar. It's right up the street. Super famous. We'll go there now. This is a good lead." Jason started walking toward it.

Bob glanced at his watch. The visit to Ben, who, he guessed, was around 60, and the sight of Darren, who couldn't have been older than 25, had made him uncomfortable. He had always been queasy around the seamier side of gay life —and straight life, for that matter—and he didn't like bars. He hated the idea of young men or women being exploited, seeking protection from older men because they couldn't rely on their families or anyone else.

All he wanted was to head home, but he knew they needed to check out what they had just heard.

The Boom Boom Room was in a ramshackle building right on the edge of the ocean, with an entrance off a side street. A few young men were outside holding plastic cups, talking, flirting, laughing, and a few more were sitting on the rocks overlooking the beach.

The bar was busy with an after-work crowd, men in suits mixing with others in . . . as little as possible. Donna Summer, the gay diva of the moment, was playing on the jukebox.

Bob hated her.

As they walked up to the bar, Bob noticed how much attention Jason immediately got. There was a look, Bob knew, that many gay men had perfected. A gaze. Brief but intense.

"What'll it be, handsome?" the bartender asked.

"Two Calistogas," Jason said, naming California's home-grown mineral water.

When the bartender returned, Jason took out his wallet, paid for the drinks, and showed the bartender his police ID.

"Well, I do declare," the bartender said in a fake Southern accent. "The law has arrived."

Jason explained that they were looking into a murder, that the bar was not in trouble in any way, and asked if he could show the bartender a photo.

"Sure," he said, throwing his towel over his shoulder.

The bartender studied it for a moment.

"Yeah, he's been here a few times. A business type. Expensive suit."

"Did you ever see him leave with anyone?"

The bartender hesitated.

"Please," Bob said, "the man was murdered. We need your help."

"I remember once he was being chatted up by Richie."

"What do you know about this Richie?" Jason asked.

"He used to do porn. His porn name was Matt something-or-other. You know porn names. Now I think he sometimes works for . . ."

The bartender hesitated again.

"For Ben?" Jason offered.

"Yeah. For Ben."

"How long ago did you see them together?"

"Hard to say. So many people in and out. Maybe four months? Something like that."

"Do you know where this Richie lives?"

"No, sorry. And I can't imagine him killing anyone. He's a gentle soul."

"Thanks. You've been very helpful." Jason gave him a card and asked him to call if he remembered anything else.

Jason and Bob both took quick swigs of their drinks and left. They walked back to Ben's, but there was no answer at the door.

"Shit," Jason said.

Back on the street, Jason walked straight to a pay phone down the block. He took out a small pad and dialed a number.

"Ben, this is Detective Thompson. We need a phone number and address for one of your escorts. Real name Richie. He used to do porn. Please call me at the number on my card as soon as possible."

"I'm tempted," Jason said, "to stick around to see if Ben returns. But you probably need to get back."

"Yeah, I kinda do."

"It's okay. If Ben has any info, we can get it over the phone."

They hit rush hour traffic on the drive back to San Diego.

Neither of them said much at first.

Jason finally said, "Do you think Amy knew about Sam?"

"I don't know. Maybe. If she didn't know, she must have suspected. I mean, she started the affair with Fred."

"Hmm."

"Why do you think," Bob asked, changing the subject, "the local police haven't shut down Ben's business?"

"Well, people are going to sell themselves no matter what you do, so a lot of us think there's not much point in trying to prevent it, unless other crimes are involved—sex trafficking, drugs, violence of some kind."

"So . . . look the other way?"

"Yeah. Also, it's a question of resources. Most police forces are stretched thin. Really thin. You have to decide what's most important."

Bob mulled that over. Jason, too, seemed lost in thought.

Traffic was murder when they reached the outskirts of San Diego.

64

They got back downtown around 7:00. As soon as Jason dropped him off Bob went straight to his car and drove home. He was exhausted.

Marcus was sitting in the living room with his arms folded over his chest. Bob went over to the couch and kissed him.

"What is it? What's wrong?"

"We're being watched."

"What?"

"There's a car across the street. The Buick. I've noticed it before but it didn't register. Until today. There's a guy sitting behind the wheel reading a newspaper. Always the same guy. He just sits there."

Bob walked over to the living room window and saw the car. He tried not to panic.

"Maybe it's not us."

Marcus gave him a sideways glance.

"Well, who knows," Bob said. "He could be a private detective hired by someone to watch their husband, or wife, to see if they're having an affair. Or something like that. We don't know the neighbors. It could be anything. A child custody dispute. Who knows."

"Can you get your new friends at the police department to see what's what? This is giving me the creeps."

"Okay, sure, I'll mention it. Still, there's no reason for the police to be watching me. I'm working with them." He hoped he sounded convincing, though he was beginning to panic.

Marcus's face relaxed a little.

"What are we doing about dinner?"

"Turns out there's an Italian place that delivers. I picked up a menu." Marcus got up to get it.

"Order anything. I'm going to take a shower."

In the bedroom he grabbed a pad and pen, went to the window, and wrote down the Buick's license plate number.

By the time they finished dinner and cleaned up it was after 9:00, and they both felt gloomy as well as tired. Before getting into bed Bob called Perez at home. He told him what was going on and gave him the license number.

"Who could it be?" Bob asked.

"I don't know. It's not SDPD. I'm sure of that."

"Well, it's someone, and I want to know who. And why."

"I'm on it."

65

Perez was waiting for Bob when he got to the office at 9:15. He followed Bob in and shut the door behind him.

"The car is registered to the Secret Service."

"I beg your pardon?" Bob thought Perez was trying to make a joke.

"The car watching your house is registered to the Secret Service. Apparently, they're in town at the mayor's request. When Sam was killed, the White House offered her additional protection, and she accepted."

Bob felt like he had been slapped. Hard.

"Is that even legal? Using the Secret Service like that?"

"Probably not."

"And why are they watching *me*?"

"My guess is that your boss told the mayor you were pushing hard on investigating the marriage, and Sam's personal life." Perez looked down at the floor and clearly did not want to look up.

Bob's mind was racing. "What good does it do her to have me watched at home?"

"I don't know what they're thinking. Or what she's thinking. She may think you're somehow working for her political enemies. I don't know."

"So I got a job with the San Diego DA just in case her husband got killed?"

"Makes no sense, I know. Or maybe she's hoping to intimidate you in some way. Hard to say. She may not be rational at this point."

Bob tried hard to bring his breathing back to normal.

After a moment he stood up and started pacing.

"So what do we do?" he finally said.

Perez shrugged. "There are a couple of options. Number one, I go to Fred, threaten to expose this, and he takes care of it. I'm willing to do that."

"Go on."

"Number two, we confront the mayor when we interview her tomorrow. We maybe should do that anyway."

"Okay."

"Option three, we do nothing. By tomorrow's interview, the mayor will know that it's not just you interested in the details of the marriage, or Sam's sex life, it's now central to the investigation."

Bob's mind was still racing. "How could Fred do this? He's the DA, for Chrissake! He's supposed to uphold the law, not break it."

"We don't know if Fred did anything more than discuss the case with Amy, which is bad enough, of course."

"How can I keep working for someone who arranged for me to be spied on?"

Perez hesitated. "I can't answer that for you. And, remember, it's just a theory. We don't have any proof."

Bob sat back down.

"I need to think. I'm going to tell them I'm sick and go home."

"There's that interview today with Cunningham's ex-wife. And Thompson probably will want to follow up on Laguna Beach."

"I'm sure you can get along without me.

"Look, I'm sorry about this. It's a hell of a thing to happen, I know."

"Well, at least I know. Thanks for your help. What time

tomorrow do we talk to the mayor? I want to be there, and we should connect before it starts."

"Eleven o'clock at HQ."

"Okay, I'll be there half an hour before."

"Meet me at that little coffee shop down the block first."

"Yeah, okay, good idea."

Perez smiled a thin smile and left.

Bob went to find Cathy. He rubbed his forehead, and said he had a fever, and was going home.

"Poor baby," she answered. "Lots of fluids!"

66

Marcus wasn't home; Bob remembered that he was planning to go up to campus and use the library for the day. He took off his suit, put on shorts and a T-shirt, and went into the kitchen. He poured a tiny bit of vodka into a glass of orange juice and gulped it down. It burned.

He stared at the telephone. He picked up the receiver and dialed his father's office. When he reached Jacob he told him what he had heard from Perez.

"Unbelievable. That mayor is something."

"So is my boss. So what do I do?"

"I need to think this through. Let me call you later today."

"Okay. Thanks Dad. By the way, I'm home. I said I was sick."

"And try to stay calm."

"Calm. Right. Fat chance."

They hung up.

The vodka was making Bob sleepy. He lay down on the

unmade bed and quickly fell asleep, and didn't wake up until the phone rang at 12:30. It was Jason.

"Hey. Are you okay?"

"Yeah, just a little under the weather."

"Well, take care of yourself. I tracked down Richie through a friend in the Vice Squad in the Valley." The San Fernando Valley in Los Angeles was the heart of the porn industry.

"He died a couple of months ago in San Francisco. AIDS."

"Ahh."

"I'm going to talk to some more bartenders here in town today, and a few of the locals involved in gay porn."

"Good idea."

"Are you sure you're okay? You sound funny."

"I'll be fine. Just a summer cold I think."

"Okay. I'll check in later, or tomorrow."

Bob made himself a peanut butter and jelly sandwich and drank what was left of the breakfast coffee. Then he wandered out to the patio and tried to think clearly about what was happening.

He couldn't think, he realized. He was too angry.

He remembered he had once been told by a friend who was studying to be a psychologist that anger was often a cover for other emotions, such as humiliation or disappointment or fear.

At the moment, he didn't care. He wanted to hold on to his anger.

He went back inside and started cleaning the bathroom, then the kitchen, then the living room. He polished the dining room table. He wanted to tire himself out.

He noticed the Buick had reappeared.

Around 3:00 his father called.

"Okay, here's what I think you should do. Have the detective—Perez?—talk to Duane, not Fred. Duane should confront Fred. If he won't, Perez can talk to Fred directly, but I'm betting Duane will do his duty."

"Okay."

"Fred has to be confronted. And putting him on the spot is the only way to find out if he actually wanted you watched, or knew it was happening."

"Yeah. Makes sense."

"Try to keep an open mind. He may not have known, in which case he's guilty of terrible judgment in blabbing to Amy, but not guilty of having any great animus toward you. We already know he wasn't happy that you were pushing to find out more about Sam's personal life, so that's not really a surprise."

"And I just go on working here as if nothing had happened?"

"We cross that bridge when we know more. And it wouldn't hurt for the police to let the mayor know they're on to her scheme. Puts her on the defensive."

"I guess that makes sense. Thanks Dad. I don't know what I'd do without you."

"Well, then you'd have to rely on your brother."

They both laughed as they hung up.

A few minutes later Adelman the accountant called.

"I hear you're sick."

"I'll be fine."

"Good. I just wanted to give you a quick update. Couldn't find Duane, he's is in court. We've been through all of the mayor's bank and finance records. There is no trace of a large sum of cash being withdrawn that could have paid off a hit man. We went back eighteen months. Nothing."

"I see."

"Of course, that doesn't mean she didn't have enough cash in a safe or a safe deposit box somewhere, but there's no way to trace that."

"Right, of course. Thanks."

"Sure thing. Take care."

Bob called Cathy and reported what he had just heard from Adelman.

Around 4:30, Marcus came home.

"Pooh, what are you doing home?"

"Having a nervous breakdown."

67

B ob gave Marcus a rundown of the day.

"Jesus Christ. The Secret Service."

"Yeah."

"Do you think Fred knew? Or is this Amy? Maybe she wanted you to know you were being watched."

"Maybe. I don't know about Fred. And I don't know if he'll be honest when Duane or Perez talk to him. I . . ."

"What?"

"I don't trust him."

Marcus let that sink in.

"Okay, look. Dad is right. One step at a time. We found out what's going on. That's the most important thing."

"I guess so."

"And besides. I took a good look at the guy in the Buick. He's kinda cute. In a Kirk Douglas sort of way."

"Maybe we should invite him in for a drink."

Marcus got up and grabbed Bob's arm.

"Where are we going?" Bob asked.

"To the bedroom. Sex will take your mind off things. Then we're going to that place in Ocean Beach for dinner. Then tomorrow you'll see what's what."

Bob smiled and followed Marcus.

68

The next morning, he skipped going to the office at 9:00 in favor of meeting Perez at the coffee shop. He was surprised to find Duane and the police chief with him.

"Bob, Perez filled me in," Duane said before Bob was fully seated. "I'm so sorry about this. I had no idea. Truly. It's beyond outrageous."

"Neither did I," Murphy muttered.

Bob realized Perez had the same instinct as his father: Let Duane do the dirty work. And he talked to his boss, too. I guess that's only natural, he thought to himself. Everybody reports to someone.

"We confronted Fred first thing this morning," Duane continued. "The Chief and I. He feels terrible. I've actually never seen him so upset. He swears he did not know Amy was using the Secret Service this way. He thought they were only going to be in California for a couple of days after Sam got killed, during the funeral and so forth."

"I see," Bob said, keeping his voice even. He didn't know if he believed Fred's story.

"This use of the Secret Service is blatantly illegal," Murphy said. "And they always connect with the local police when they're in town. Always." Murphy sounded genuinely angry.

"We're going to confront Amy. She needs to explain herself. It's a hard way to get it, but this gives us leverage over her. It may shake some truth out of her about Sam."

"I'm so glad to be of use," Bob said with barely hidden sarcasm.

"Look," Duane went on, "I know you're pissed off. You have every right to be. Probably wondering whether you want to go on working for the DA. I would be, too. But we're going to handle this. We will protect you."

"And," Murphy added, "if we have to, we can leak the story to the press. Amy will know that could happen. It could derail her career. Not to mention explode in D.C. She'll play ball."

"Well," Bob said, "okay. Let's see what she says."

They got up and walked over to police headquarters. Walking along the sidewalk, four abreast, Bob couldn't help but think of a Hollywood Western. Some of the people next to him, he said to himself, probably even had guns.

69

As they approached the police building, they saw a large tangle of reporters, cameras, and television trucks. Reporters with microphones rushed up to them.

"Chief Murphy, why are you interviewing the mayor?"

Bob was impressed: Murphy did not lose his cool. He, Duane, and Perez stood behind the Chief.

"As you know, Mayor Berkman's husband was brutally murdered. Our investigation is intense and ongoing. It is routine to speak to a spouse in a tragic situation such as this."

"Do you have any suspects?"

"You know, Randy, that I won't comment on an investigation still in progress. We have leads and we are pursuing them."

"Is the mayor a suspect?"

"No, she is not. That's all for now, we have work to do."

They proceeded into the building, with reporters firing questions after them, including one very loud reporter who shouted, "Why are you doing this interview here?"

No one said anything until they reached the interview room adjacent to the chief's office on the top floor. Bob took his place outside the two-way mirror. The other three entered the room, where Bobbitt was already waiting.

Bob was impressed that Duane was going to sit in on the interview and not just observe. *Maybe he means business*, he thought to himself.

Jason joined Bob in front of the mirror. *God*, Bob told himself, *he really does look like Tab Hunter*.

"Nothing yet from the locals," Jason said quietly. "I don't think Sam did much in town. At least not in the usual places."

"Mmm," was the only comment Bob could muster.

A few minutes later, Amy Berkman, accompanied by Sandy Nelson, entered the room from the other side. Everyone stood. Amy clearly had dressed for the meeting, in an elegant blue suit, pearls, and heels, and she was wearing heavy makeup; the kind of makeup a woman would wear who knew she might be photographed or on camera.

"You all know Sandy Nelson, my chief of staff."

Everyone nodded as they took their seats. Nelson poured himself and Amy glasses of water from the carafe in the middle of the table.

Murphy began.

"Mayor Berkman, you were given Secret Service protection at the time of your husband's death. Is that correct?"

"Yes. President Bush was kind enough to offer me extra security at the time."

"Then, may I ask why are they still here?"

Amy paused briefly. "Because you still have not found out who murdered my husband, and whether the murder is connected in some way to my office."

Duane spoke up; his voice was cold and strident.

"Then can you tell us why a Secret Service agent has been asked to observe the home of Bob Abramson, an Assistant District Attorney, who is working on the case under my supervision?"

Amy took a sip of water. Bob thought he detected a slight tremble in her hand.

"I had no idea they were there."

"You had no idea," Murphy repeated.

"No."

"So," Duane said, "they just happened to appear in front of Mr. Abramson's home in Normal Heights, day after day?"

Sandy Nelson said, "Why don't you ask them?"

"Because," Murphy said, "we're asking you. Your answer is not credible, Mayor Berkman. So here's what's going to happen. When you leave this meeting, you will call the White House and tell them that you no longer need extra protection and ask that all agents be recalled. All of them. If they are not recalled within twenty-four hours, you will find the story of the illegal use of the Secret Service on the front page of every major newspaper in the country."

Amy looked straight at Murphy.

"Do not threaten me."

"I'm not threatening you, ma'am. I'm telling you what you need to do, and what will happen if you don't. If you need additional security, which I very much doubt, the San Diego Police Department will be glad to provide it."

Amy swallowed. "Is there anything else?"

Well, well, well, Bob thought, this was a woman who knew how to cut her losses. The sign of a good politician. She could go far.

"Yes," Duane said. "We're just getting started. You've previously told us that the money Sam deposited in a bank in Switzerland was for European property development."

"Yes."

"We have had forensic accountants going through Sam's records, and we find absolutely no trace, no mention, of such a project or projects. His staff was unaware of any such plans as well. Can you explain that?"

"No, I cannot. Perhaps it was just something in Sam's head. As I told you, I didn't know the details of his business."

"And you are sticking to your story that you knew about the funds?"

"It's not a story, Duane," Amy said icily. "It's the truth."

Murphy asked her, "Do you have a safe at your home?"

"A safe? No."

"Do you have a safe deposit box?"

"Yes."

"What does it contain? I should warn you that we are prepared to get a subpoena to open the box."

"There's no need of that. It contains documents, the deed to the house in La Jolla, that sort of thing, and a few pieces of jewelry left to me by my mother. I intend to pass them along to my daughter some day. I'll be glad to open it for you."

"And no cash?"

"No."

"Has there ever been cash in the box?"

"No."

"When was the last time you visited the box?"

"I have no idea. Years."

Sandy Nelson was taking notes on a small pad he had taken from his suitcoat pocket.

Perez took notes as well. Now he looked up and asked, "How long has your affair with Fred Stevens been going on?"

Bob was impressed. Quickly changing the subject, he knew, was a good way to throw a witness off balance.

Amy looked rattled.

"We're leaving," Nelson said. He started to stand.

"No, it's all right," she said to Nelson, who reluctantly sat back down. "We've been seeing each other for several years. We're really just good friends at this point."

Perez held her in his gaze. "Did the affair start because of your husband's sexual preferences?"

Bob winced, but in this context, he thought, it made sense to use the term.

Amy looked down. She knew she needed to answer. Again, Bob thought, this is a smart woman.

"Yes."

"And did you know that Gerald Otley in New York worked as an escort, for both men and women?"

"I did not know, but I suspected as much when I heard about the bequest in Sam's will."

Amy put her hands on the table.

"You have to understand something," she went on. "Sam and I had two children. They're quite young. They loved their father. I was trying to protect them."

"And," Duane said, "protect your political future."

Amy stared at him. "If that's what you believe, Duane, nothing I can say will make any difference."

"Is Sam Daniel's biological father?" Duane asked.

"I beg your pardon?"

"It's a simple question. Was your husband Daniel's biological father?"

"I'm not going to answer that."

"We could put you under oath, one way or another."

"Fine. Go ahead. And I'll sue you for invasion of privacy."

"You have no privacy, Amy, you're a public official," Duane said with a half smile, "and this is a murder investigation. You might want to check Supreme Court precedent on that, especially if the information is true. Is it true?"

Amy stared at him and said nothing. It seemed like no one in the room was breathing.

Murphy broke the impasse.

"As far as you were aware, was Sam actively involved with someone here in town who might have wanted him dead?"

"We didn't talk about these things. We led our separate personal lives. But my sense is that when Sam wanted to see someone, he did so out of town."

"Where?"

"I don't know."

"Did Sam have a separate residence somewhere?"

"Not to my knowledge."

"We know," Perez said, "that he was involved with a young man in Laguna Beach. That young man has since died of AIDS. As far as you were aware, was there any chance Sam was infected?"

"One of the few things I insisted on," Amy says, "was that Sam be as careful as possible about his health. So I very much doubt it."

"He had no symptoms of illness?"

"No, none."

"Did he know his HIV status?"

"Not as far as I was aware."

"Did Sam ever discuss divorce?" Duane asked.

"No. Never."

"Did you have a pre-nuptial agreement of any kind?"

"No."

"If Sam was thinking of divorce, it could explain the money in Switzerland."

"I've answered your questions about that."

Everyone was quiet for several moments. The men stared at Amy and she stared back at them.

After nearly a full minute, she stood up. "If this inquisition is over, gentlemen, I'll be going."

"Don't leave town," Murphy said. "And don't forget the call you need to make."

"Not leave town? Am I a suspect?"

"Not at this time. That could change."

At the door, Amy turned around. "Good day. *Gentlemen.*" She and Nelson walked out; Bob noticed that her composure was perfect, no doubt for the photographers waiting outside. Nelson, on the other hand, seemed to be very angry.

70

The three interrogators came through the opposite door to join Bob in the viewing area. They followed Murphy to his office conference table.

"Well?" Murphy said, looking around.

"I think she's lying about the Swiss money," Duane said, "but we have no way to prove it. I don't think she's lying about the safe deposit box. Too easy to check. And I'm betting she'll make the call to the White House."

Perez said he'd check the bank to see if Amy had visited the box recently.

"I thought it was interesting," Murphy said, "that she wouldn't answer the question about Daniel. What made you ask?"

"Well, the affair with Fred has been going on for a long time. Daniel is young."

"I had the same thought," Bob said, "after meeting Daniel, that day at the house. Something about him reminded me of Fred."

"Well," Murphy said, "that's their business, unless it somehow becomes relevant to the case. But we do need to know if the affair really has cooled, as Amy said. You'll have to ask Fred. Find out where they met, how often, all of that."

Duane didn't look happy, but he mumbled, "All right."

"I don't see her arranging the murder," Murphy continued. "There's no money trail, and it sounds like they had worked out an arrangement that suited both of them. It happens. Especially in politics. And she's ambitious. Very ambitious."

"What about her security detail?"

"We've talked to them all, taken their prints," Murphy said. "No match to Mr. X. And all of them have alibis that check out for the time of the murder."

Murphy turned to Perez. "Did you get anything out of Cunningham's ex? What's her name?"

"Judith Powers, and no, not really. She said they married too young, didn't grow in the same direction, the usual talk-show bullshit. When we pushed her, she admitted that Cunningham could be a bit rough in the bedroom, but nothing more than that. And we already knew that from that lawyer friend of his, Lucy Hargrave."

Perez looked as though the thought of "intense" sex, as Hargrave had described their encounters, upset him. *He must be a good Catholic*, Bob told himself. He couldn't help wondering what Perez thought of his and Marcus's relationship.

Murphy sighed. "Okay. Then we have no reason to question Cunningham again. Thompson needs to dig more into Sam's private life. With you, Bob, if you're still on the case."

Everyone turned toward him.

"I'm still in. For now. And I appreciate your taking a hard line on the Secret Service. What do you think she was trying to accomplish by watching me?"

"Something occurred to me during the interview," Murphy said. "It could be it was Sandy Nelson who had them watching you, and she really didn't know. It's possible."

He went on, "She clearly tells him everything—and relies on him to keep some things from her. What's the phrase? 'Plausible deniability.' I imagine he doesn't tell her everything."

"Or maybe it was Amy," he sighed. "We'll probably never know. But my guess is that they were hoping to get some dirt on you. Either that, or they wanted you to know you were being watched so it would scare you."

"Well, it did."

"Think of it this way," Duane said. "You now have a potent weapon against her if she tries to retaliate. So do I. So does Chief Murphy. She knows that. Fred knows that. They're not going to mess with you. Neither one of them."

Bob felt only nominally better as the meeting broke up.

71

Jason was waiting for him in the hallway; he suggested they talk about their next steps over lunch. Bob told Duane he'd be in his office later that afternoon.

Jason drove them to California Cuisine in Hillcrest, where they asked for a corner table on the patio so they wouldn't be overheard. After they ordered Bob gave him a quick summary of the meeting with Amy. Jason told him he had set up interviews over the next few days with some of the names on Amy's list of Sam's friends.

"And," Jason said, "I think we have to go up to LA, show Sam's pictures around the bars there. Especially since Amy says Sam usually went out of town to fool around. We may need to fly up to San Francisco, especially if Sam's records show he spent time there. He's from there originally, right?"

Bob nodded.

After lunch, Bob was at his desk when Duane stopped in to say that Fred confirmed Amy's story that the affair had cooled. He'd also agreed to give the accountants his credit card receipts. They were already going through Amy's, looking for charges from hotels, motels, and other places.

Bob closed the door behind Duane and called his father. He gave him a quick summary of what had transpired.

"Well, okay. It sounds like Duane and the police chief are backing you up."

"The police chief is a by-the-book guy, thank God. But Duane. And Fred. I mean, my God. They both withheld information from a murder investigation."

"They made mistakes."

"Mistakes?! I mean, what they both did, especially the DA, it's pretty close to obstruction of justice."

"Okay, yes. Fair enough."

"How can I stay here?"

"I understand how you feel. I would feel the same way. But maybe wait a while to make a decision about staying. Most of the day-to-day supervision of the ADAs is through Duane, right? And he'll be contrite. You probably can mostly avoid Fred."

"Yeah, I guess so. But I don't know, Dad. I don't know if I can work for these people. This is pretty serious corruption. This is the DA's office. We're supposed to be the good guys, you know, find the bad guys, protect the public." Bob paused for a moment. "I mean . . ."

"What?"

"A man was murdered in cold blood, but these guys were interested in protecting their secrets. Out of self-interest."

"Well, yes . . ."

"Fred wanted to keep his affair secret and to protect his lover. And incidentally, to run for her job when she moves up. And Duane wanted to stay in his boss's good graces, and, probably, take over as DA. Self-interest. Stands to reason."

"Welcome to the real world, Bobby. Why do you think I work in a really small office, just two of us?"

It took a moment for to that sink in.

Bob swallowed. "I thought the law would be different."

"It can be. Give it a chance. Give the job some time. See where the case goes, how they react to you. Pass the bar. Then you have options."

"Thanks, Dad. I'll be . . . patient. You're the best," he said before hanging up.

He left the office early so he could eat before going

out to a meeting Jason had set up for 8:00 p.m. Over an early dinner he told Marcus everything, including what his father had advised. Marcus breathed a sigh of relief when Bob told him the Secret Service was gone for good, but he didn't say much until Bob was clearly finished, and asked, "So what do I do?"

Marcus ruminated for a moment. At moments like these, Bob knew, his professor side came out.

"'Ambition must be made to counteract ambition.'"

"What?"

"James Madison, in the Federalist. He was writing about how the government would have to be set up, given human nature. And he wrote, 'Ambition must be made to counteract ambition.'"

"And this is relevant because . . .?"

"Because you're dealing with three very, very ambitious people. So you need to decide what you want for yourself when this case is over."

Bob looked at Marcus and nodded. He wanted to talk more, but he had to dress for the meeting with Sam's friend.

72

Peter Davidson lived in a large condo in La Jolla just steps from the beach. He was what Bob would call a well-preserved older man in his fifties. It looked like he frequented the gym and possibly had had a face-lift and a hair transplant. His story was that he had first run into Sam at a gay bar in Los Angeles. They became friends, and, Davidson said, he gave Sam some pointers on how to discreetly have a gay life while married to a woman, a situation Davidson himself had been in for a decade.

That interview, and talks with Sam's other friends over the next few days, revealed little beyond confirming Amy's version of Sam's personal life. Some of the men were openly gay; with others, it was hard to tell, and they didn't reveal much at all. Several were golf partners. One was an old friend of Sam's from his years in graduate school at Wharton in Philadelphia.

Most of them were attractive, tan and fit, and Bob noticed that many of them flirted with Jason. Jason said that a few looked familiar, presumably from gay venues, but only in a "sort-of" way. They visited a series of luxurious condos and houses in La Jolla and in the beach neighborhoods of San Diego and the towns to the north.

The one interview that revealed some useful information was with Jeffrey Kahn, Sam's architect and golfing partner. Kahn acknowledged that he and Sam had been intimate the morning of his death, the morning he'd visited the house for a supposed golf date. Sam's knee really was bothering him, which is why they didn't play golf, and, Kahn said with a rueful smile, one thing led to another. He revealed that Sam and Amy slept in separate rooms, and that, as far as he could tell, Amy was fully aware of Sam's other life.

"Sam had a hard time admitting, even to himself, that he was attracted to men," Kahn said. "I mean, here he was, ensconced in a very public marriage, with kids. It can't have been easy."

"Do you know if he was entertaining the idea of divorce?"

"No, I'm pretty sure he wasn't. At least, as far as I knew. At least not while the kids were young. Sam really did love them. And he cared for Amy, and wanted her to succeed in politics. I don't think he would have done anything to hurt her."

Kahn had left for a business trip to Denver the afternoon Sam died, and gave them the names of the hotel and the people he met there. They scratched him off the list: he had no motive, no opportunity, and an airtight alibi.

Once they had gone through Amy's list, Bob and Marcus arranged to stay with Alex and Carol in Los Angeles for a few days while Bob and Jason visited some gay venues in LA and made inquiries.

73

Alex and Carol lived in Santa Monica, not far from the ocean, in a large shingled house they had bought when their son was born. There was a small guest suite over their garage. The moment Bob and Marcus walked into the main house was happy bedlam: Jay greeted them with hugs and squeals while Sophie danced around them barking with joy.

"Come see the puppies, Uncle Bob," Jay said, grabbing him by the arm.

The puppies were kept in a small pantry off the kitchen, and Sophie was the epitome of the proud momma. She wagged and wagged her tail. Bob immediately got down on the ground so the puppies could climb all over him. Marcus knew there was no point in trying to argue that maybe a puppy wasn't such a great idea.

"Which are the boys?" Bob asked Carol, laughing.

"Um, the ones with blue ribbons."

"Ah, gender stereotyping in the animal kingdom," Marcus said, as he crouched down and Sophie licked his face.

"This one," Bob said, "this is Oscar Wilde." Bob

handed Oscar to Marcus, who lifted him up, looked him in the eye, and said "Young man, you will be well behaved, or you will be sorry."

Later, over iced tea in the garden, Bob explained to Carol what he was doing in LA, skirting her questions about the case. When Alex came home from work they enjoyed a leisurely dinner in the garden.

Jay asked Bob to read him his bedtime story. "You can come too, Uncle Marcus," he added.

Bob and Marcus smiled at each other.

Over the next two days Marcus visited colleagues at UCLA and USC while Bob and Jason spent the afternoons and evenings touring the gay bars in West Hollywood and Silver Lake, two of the gayest neighborhoods in the country. They showed Sam's pictures to bar owners and bartenders, and though one or two said Sam looked somewhat familiar, nobody could provide any details.

"We're not getting anywhere," Jason finally said, adding that they needed to check sex clubs and bathhouses. Bob reluctantly agreed.

They spent an evening doing so, and no one recognized Sam's picture. Bob was deeply depressed by what he saw at these places. They were in dilapidated buildings with little ventilation, humid, fetid, with men who looked like they were drunk or high, some of them no doubt spreading HIV. After each visit, he was grateful to get back outside in the fresh air.

"Why doesn't the city close down these places?" he asked.

"They tried. It's kinda pointless. They just reopen somewhere else. They become 'private' clubs, but you can walk in and buy a membership for a single night."

"I see."

"At least," Jason said, "they can hand out condoms in a

place like that. You can't do that in a park."

They left for home the next morning. Early that afternoon Bob reported to Duane, who told him the accountants had been through Fred's credit card receipts for several years, and they seemed to confirm what Fred had told them about the affair. For a while there had been brief stays in hotels and resorts, and they became less and less frequent over time.

"Of course, they could have been meeting somewhere else," Duane said, "but we have no way of knowing. And Fred swears things had cooled off. And he's still contrite. I think he'd tell me the truth at this point."

The accountants didn't find much in Sam's credit card receipts, except for one possible clue: Several trips to San Francisco in the last year, with stays at the Fairmount Hotel.

"You and Jason should fly up there. See what you can dig up."

They left the next day. Bob was beginning to feel dizzy from all the traveling.

"California is too damned big," he said to Marcus as he packed another suitcase.

74

The moment they stepped off the plane, Bob couldn't believe he was in the same state; it was freezing.

"First law of California weather," Jason said. "San Francisco is always cold. Especially in summer." A fierce wind was coming off the bay, and the city was shrouded in fog as their rented car made its way into the city. Bob could see that San Francisco had a very different feel than

San Diego or Los Angeles. It was more compact and had an almost East coast vibe, with a busy downtown. Except for the hills and cable cars, it could have been Boston.

Bob missed Boston, and, at the moment he wished he and Marcus had never left.

They checked into the Fairmount, an elegant old hotel on Nob Hill, a posh neighborhood full of stately homes, many of them restored Victorians. Duane had agreed they could stay there if they shared a room.

They began by talking to the hotel staff, one or two of whom said that yes, Sam looked familiar. All claimed that, as far as they knew, he stayed alone.

They got lucky, though, with one room-service waiter.

"Yeah, he was here. He ordered from room service a lot." He hesitated. "A couple of times, Don Cade was in his room."

Finally, Bob thought, *a lead*.

Jason thought it would be risky to try to interview Cade as law enforcement officers: a popular gay porn actor who also worked as an escort, he might clam up. So they called his number and left a message, saying they'd like to arrange an "appointment" at the Fairmount.

Cade called back about a half hour later, and they arranged a meeting for that evening at 9:00. Jason gave him the room number.

"It will be a three-way, me and my boyfriend," Jason said.

"Cool. That's $1,000, cash up front."

"No problem," Jason said.

Cade arrived on time. He was brutally handsome, with black hair and green eyes and a physique he clearly cultivated, bulging in all the right places.

Jason bolted the door behind him, and then showed him his police ID; Cade immediately tried to punch him.

Jason blocked the punch and quickly had Cade pinned on the carpet.

"Look. We're not here to shake you down, or arrest you. We need information. We can do this the easy way, here, or we can do it down at SFPD and leave you with the vice squad. Up to you."

Cade stopped struggling and grunted, "Yeah, all right." He shrugged Jason off, stood up, and sat warily in the desk chair.

"We're looking into the murder of this man," Jason said, sliding a copy of Sam's picture toward him. "People here at the hotel say you've been with him."

"Yeah, a few times."

"How many?"

Cade was carefully putting his hair back in place.

"Maybe three. The first time he just wanted to talk. He was nervous, a closet case, I thought. I get a lot of those."

"And?"

"And I was surprised to hear from him again. The second time he was less nervous, and wanted what most guys like him want." Cade touched his crotch.

"Go on."

"The third time, I think, he wanted a tour of gay nightlife, so I took him to a few bars, and then we came back here."

"Do you know if he was seeing anyone else in town?"

"Dunno. He said he was from LA."

"He was from San Diego."

"Who was he?"

"Sam Berkman."

Cade showed no sign of recognizing the name.

"Married? I figured."

Bob spoke up.

"Did he ever talk to you about his family, or his business?"

"No. He said he was a lawyer and single."

"And did you practice safe sex?"

"Sex with me is never safe," Cade said, smirking. "But we used condoms, yeah."

"For the record," Jason asked, "have you been in San Diego in the last month or so?"

"No, haven't left San Francisco."

"Do you keep a calendar?"

Cade pulled a small notebook out of his coat pocket and handed it to Jason.

Bob looked over his shoulder while Jason thumbed through it. It was full of names, often just a first name or initials, many phone numbers, and some specific times. On the date of the murder, there were three appointments listed. Jason wrote down the numbers.

"All right. We appreciate your help," Jason said, handing him the notebook and a card. "Call me if you think of anything else."

Cade got up, put on his coat, and leaned over to Jason.

"Next time, big boy, call me when you're alone. We could have a lot of fun."

75

He didn't do it," Bob said. "Do you really think it's worth going to San Francisco bars? I mean, at best, it will be more of the same. A bartender might remember seeing him and might remember that he was talking to Tom, Dick, or Harry, and no, they don't know where we can reach any of them."

Jason sighed. "You're probably right, but we'll check these numbers just to make sure. In the morning I'll call the chief, and you call Duane."

Bob nodded.

"Let's get some air."

They put on their jackets and wandered around Nob Hill, stopping for coffee at a small, elegant espresso bar. Bob was still freezing and wished he had a scarf. He noticed that the people in the bar all looked prosperous, well-tended, with glowing skin.

Of course, he knew that any city of this size had its seamy side.

When they got back to the hotel, Bob took a hot shower and then Jason did the same. When he got out, wrapped in a towel, Bob saw that his chest matched the rest of him: even better than Tab Hunter.

Jason noticed Bob looking, and had a look on his face that said yes, sure, why not.

Bob sighed, and, remembered a phrase Marcus had once used as a joke.

"I'm afraid I'm not that kind of girl."

Jason smiled. "Ah, well. I didn't think so. And I really do respect your relationship. You're two lucky guys."

They went to sleep in the twin beds and flew home early the next morning.

Marcus was gone when he got back to Normal Heights, so Bob decided to go to the gym they had just joined; Marcus had gone once or twice but Bob had yet to try it out. He wrote Marcus a note and signed it "B," as he usually did.

As he was gathering his gym bag, the doorbell rang; UPS had just left a package. The return address was his parents' house in Danbury.

Bob smiled; probably another shipment of baked goods from his mother. He put the package on the kitchen table next to his note to Marcus, noticing that the package was addressed to "R. Abramson."

Then he looked at his note to Marcus.

A chill went down his spine.

76

He put his gym bag away and drove to the office. When he got there, he asked Cathy for the crime scene photos.

"By the way, the mayor's chief of staff, Sandy," Bob said while Cathy got the photographs.

"Mmm?"

"Is his first name Sanford?"

"No," Cathy said. "Alexander, I think."

"Oh, right," Bob said. "Thanks."

He continued riffling through the pictures until he found what he was looking for: a photo of the note they'd found on Sam's desk after the murder. *A @ 5*, it read.

"Cathy, do you happen to know," Bob said, glancing up and trying to sound casual, "if Sandy has a sister in Phoenix?"

"Sister? No, he's an only child. We talked about it once."

Cathy looked puzzled, but Bob cut her off before she could say anything. Keeping his voice level and calm, he asked where Duane was.

"He's with Fred, I'm pretty sure," she said.

Bob walked to Fred's office. He found the door to the inner office open. The two men were at the conference table, shuffling through files. They looked up. Duane took off his glasses.

Bob put the photo in front of them and took a deep, calming breath.

"I know who killed Sam."

77

Fred and Duane looked at the photo and then gazed up at Bob, puzzled.

"My name is Robert. Begins with an 'R'. But everyone calls me Bob. Begins with a 'B'."

Both men gave blank stares.

"I don't understand," Duane said. Fred looked impatient.

"What if 'A at 5' doesn't refer to Amy, but someone else?"

The color drained from Fred's face and he clenched the fingers of his left hand into a tight fist. "Who?"

"Sandy Nelson. First name, Alexander. That's probably on his nameplate on his desk outside of Amy's office. Not 'S' for Sandy. 'A' for Alexander. Maybe Sam didn't know him well, maybe not enough to call him Sandy. Or he wanted to keep the relationship formal. Whatever. So he wrote 'A' instead of 'S'."

Fred looked again at the photo and stood up. Duane was lost in thought. Neither of them spoke for a moment.

"I'll bet money," Bob said, "that Sandy is Mr. X. Have we checked his fingerprints?"

"No," Duane said. "We didn't. He was away, out of town, the night of the murder."

"That was a fake alibi. He told us he was visiting his sister in Phoenix."

They waited.

"He doesn't have a sister."

After a short pause Fred blurted out, "That son of a bitch. Bring him in." Fred said. "Now!" He looked thunderstruck.

"No," Duane said.

The other two men looked at him.

"I'll call Perez. They can get his prints. They can tell him it's routine, printing everyone on Amy's staff. 'For the purpose of elimination.'"

Fred looked skeptical.

"We'll know if they match by tonight. If they do, we bring him in. He'll be tired. And we'll know just how hard to push."

Fred nodded reluctantly.

"Good work, Bob." After the minutest pause, he added, "Duane, leave us alone."

Bob started to sweat.

"Look, I can imagine what you've been thinking. But I swear on the lives of my children, I had no knowledge about the Secret Service watching you. I would not have allowed it."

"Okay."

Bob knew that silence could be more intimidating than angry words; besides, he didn't know what else to say. All he wanted was to get out of Fred's office as quickly as possible; he had hoped not to face him for a while. Certainly not alone. Fred mumbled, "And as for the rest—"

Bob cut him off. Suddenly he knew exactly what he wanted to say. Even how to say it.

"Yes, the rest. With all due respect, sir, you withheld vital information from this investigation. A case could be made that you obstructed justice."

"You're right. There's no excuse. None. It's the worst mistake I've ever made."

Well, Bob thought, at least he's not denying it. Again, he stayed silent.

"I can't tell you how sorry I am," Fred rambled on, his face reddening. "I . . . Look, I wouldn't blame you if you want to leave. I promise I'll write you a stellar letter of reference. I'll show it to you in advance. Now or at any time in the future. But I hope you'll stay. You probably just solved the murder of the decade."

"I haven't decided what to do. I haven't even passed the bar. I need to do that."

"When this case is over, take time off. At full pay. Finish studying for the bar, there's a sitting for the exam in August, I think."

"There is."

"Good. Take it then. And come back after Labor Day. Or not. Up to you."

Fred stood up and offered his hand. Bob hesitated a moment, then shook it, turned away, and walked out.

78

He went back to his office and exhaled. Duane stuck his head in.

"An apology?"

"Yeah."

Duane nodded and came in, shutting the door. He sat down in front of Bob's desk.

"And?"

"And I'll think about it. He offered me time off when this case is over. I'll take the bar. Then I'll see." Suddenly he asked, "Does Nelson have a family?"

Bob realized that was a strange question at this juncture, and wasn't sure why he asked, but he wanted to shift the conversation away from the DA.

"No, he's single. Lives alone as far as I know. At first I figured he was too busy in politics to have a personal life. But now I wonder if he's just . . ." Duane paused.

"Queer?" Bob forced himself to half-smile.

"I was going to say repressed. Strict religious upbringing. Grew up poor in the Central Valley, near Fresno. Got a partial scholarship to Whittier College and worked the rest of his way through, like Nixon."

"I see."

"You got the feeling with Sandy he was always trying to prove something . . . which come to think of it, was a Nixon trait as well."

Bob let that sink in and then looked at his watch; it was 5:45. He really wanted to get out of the office.

"I can't believe I didn't think to check his alibi about being in Phoenix," Duane said in a low voice.

"Well," Bob said, "there was no reason to think he was a suspect."

"I suppose, but still . . ." Duane shook his head.

There was a long silence. Finally Bob said, "I'm going home. Call me after they print him."

He drove home, exhausted. The morning in San Francisco felt like it happened weeks before, not just a few hours.

Marcus was in the kitchen, making something that looked vaguely like tuna casserole.

"How was San Francisco?"

"Cold."

"And?"

"And I met a real live pornstar. I'll live with him when I leave you."

"Fine, fine. Whatever makes you happy. I opened Mom's package. Poppy seed cake."

Bob smiled. "She'll never know how important that cake was."

"What do you mean?"

"I'll tell you, some snowy night in front of the fire." It was a line spoken by Bette Davis in *All About Eve*. A college friend of his had joked that you know you're really gay when you start quoting Bette Davis.

Bob left the kitchen as Marcus called after him. "Hey. It doesn't snow here."

As they were sitting down to dinner, the phone rang; It was Duane. Sandy's prints were on the way to the lab.

After dinner they watched the news, then listened to Ella Fitzgerald. Right at 10:00, Duane called again.

"The prints match," he said. "Sandy is Mr. X. They're bringing him in now. Meet me at Police HQ."

Bob groaned, told Marcus he had to go back to work, and got dressed again. He wasn't sure he had ever been so tired.

The police chief and Duane were already in the viewing area at HQ.

"Great work, Bob," Murphy said. "Truly. We're idiots for not paying more attention to that note."

Bob smiled. "Well, Sam was due home around that time, then going to the fundraiser. It was a natural assumption to think the 'A' meant Amy."

Duane went into the interview room, indicating to Bob

to wait outside. A moment or two later Bobbitt and Perez escorted Nelson in and sat him at the table. Perez took the seat next to him, while Murphy slipped in after them and sat next to Duane, facing the suspect. A camera had been set up.

"Mr. Nelson," the chief said, "you have a right to an attorney—"

"I know my rights. And your detectives read them to me, like good little boys."

Murphy ignored him and continued with the Miranda warnings. It was clear he would take the lead on questioning Nelson. He asked him to sign a document acknowledging that he had been read his rights.

"Are you willing to speak to us without an attorney present?"

"Yes."

"Please sign this document so indicating."

Nelson signed it.

"Did you visit Sam Berkman's office at approximately five p.m. on the day he died?"

"Yes."

"For what purpose?"

Nelson poured himself a glass of water. "I wanted to persuade Sam to stop putting Amy in danger."

"How was he putting her in danger?"

"By his . . . homosexual activity." Nelson nearly choked on the words. "Political danger.

"And then?"

"We argued. Sam said he and Amy had an understanding and that he was always discreet. But he wasn't."

"How did you know this?" Perez asked.

"I know people. And I have a contacts in San Francisco. Sam was getting less discreet."

"And why did that upset you?"

"Because Amy is going to go far. She can go all the way to the top, really, if you ask me."

"So," Murphy said, "you argued. Then what happened?"

Nelson slowly took another drink of water.

"The argument became heated. And somewhat physical. Sam knocked that glass out of my hand. Then I left."

"You left."

"Yes."

"And Sam was alive when you left?"

"Yes." Nelson said it, but without any conviction, Bob thought.

"Did Mayor Berkman know of your visit to her husband?"

"No. Absolutely not." It was the first time Nelson sounded agitated.

"Why have you not told us about this visit before?"

"Isn't it obvious?"

"Please answer the question."

Nelson hesitated. "I don't think I should say any more without a lawyer."

Murphy and Perez sat back in their chairs.

"That's your right. Please stand up."

Bobbitt walked to the table. Nelson stood. The chief nodded to his detectives.

"Alexander Nelson, I am arresting you on suspicion of first-degree murder."

Perez read the Miranda warnings again as Bobbitt put him in handcuffs.

"Is that really necessary?"

"Yes, Mr. Nelson, we handcuff murderers here in California," Murphy said.

Nelson shut his eyes for a moment. When he opened

them, he looked shriveled.

"Gentlemen," Duane said to the others, "leave us alone for a minute."

The detectives looked skeptical, but after a nod from Murphy they came out and joined Bob behind the mirror.

Duane got up and turned off the speaker in the wall and pulled down the venetian blind. He turned back to Nelson.

"Was it really worth it, Sandy? Look, we're alone, it's off the record. They can't hear us."

Nelson smiled, mostly to himself. "For where Amy is going? I'd do anything."

"And she's going to take you with her? Are you sure?"

A blank look fell over Nelson's face.

79

Alexander Nelson was arraigned for first-degree murder at 9:00 the next morning. Bob, Duane, Murphy, and Perez were in the courtroom.

He was accompanied by Sidney Carter, who had acted as James Cunningham's attorney as well. Bob thought that was strange, but no one said anything about it.

The courtroom was overrun with reporters, and the judge had to gavel them to silence three times. He read out the indictment.

"How do you plead?"

"Not guilty."

The judge again gavelled the crowd silent. "I'll hear the people on bail."

Fred was appearing for the prosecution.

"We request remand, your honor. The defendant has a passport and the means to flee. We are just a few miles from an international border. The crime could not be more serious."

Carter spoke up.

"These charges are without foundation. My client has never been accused of a crime, not so much as a parking ticket. We request ROR."

"Denied," the judge said without hesitation. "Bail is set at $10 million. The defendant will surrender his passport."

"We wish to notify the court," Fred said, "that we will be seeking the death penalty."

Bob was watching Nelson. His body froze; his head drooped and his shoulders folded inward; he had the posture of a chastised, but terrified, child. The reporters erupted, then several of them made a dash for the door. The judge furiously banged his gavel.

Bob assumed that Fred announced the death penalty to put pressure on Nelson to strike a deal of some sort. Clever move, he thought. He wondered if it would work.

"Trial date, October 9. Next case."

The courtroom emptied out.

On the steps of the courthouse, a makeshift podium had appeared. The police chief and the DA walked up to it. Uniformed police officers were keeping reporters a discreet distance away, although they kept trying to surge forward.

"We have every reason to believe," Fred said, "that we have arrested the right man for this heinous crime. We're confident of conviction."

Both men left the podium as reporters shouted questions after them.

Bob went home and slept most of the rest of the day.

80

Mayor Berkman held a press conference later that afternoon. Bob and Marcus watched clips of it on the six-o'clock local news.

Amy met the press in a small auditorium at City Hall. She wore the same blue suit and pearls she had had on during her second interrogation. She appeared shaken but composed.

"Good afternoon." She paused. "Thank you for coming on short notice. The charges in this case are, of course, serious. I have faith in the San Diego police and in the District Attorney's office."

She paused to take a drink of water from a glass that had been placed under the podium.

"I would remind everyone that in this country, the accused is innocent until proven guilty. Mr. Nelson, who has served my administration loyally, deserves a fair trial, as any citizen would."

She held tightly to the sides of the podium. Though her hands shook and her knuckles were white, her voice was firm and she spoke slowly.

"I wish to state categorically that I had absolutely no knowledge of how my husband was killed, or by whom. I ask the good citizens of San Diego and all of California to be patient as the judicial process moves forward, and to give my family time to recover from these tragic events."

Amy turned and left without taking questions. Reporters shouted after her. The news cameras lingered long enough to hear two questions.

"How could you not know, Amy?"

"Did he tell you, Amy?"

The story got a brief mention halfway through the CBS national evening news at 6:30.

"So," Marcus asked, "what do you think? Did she know?"

"I don't know."

"Come on, you must have an opinion."

"Actually, I don't. If she did, we'll find out. Nelson will use it to cut some kind of deal and avoid the gas chamber. Maybe."

81

Over the weekend, Bob took Marcus to his office for the first time; together they packed up his bar briefing books and lugged them home. Bob set himself up on the dining room table, and within a few days he was able to buckle down and concentrate. He tried not to think about the case.

Ten days later Duane called.

"I thought you'd want an update," Duane said.

"Not really," Bob said. "But give it to me anyway."

"Well, we think Sandy may cut a deal, pleading guilty to second degree. He seems to be weakening."

"Mmm."

"What I don't think we're going to hear is anything implicating the mayor."

"I'm not surprised."

"Really? I am, at least a little."

"What is the usual sentence for second degree?"

"Fifteen years to life."

"What do you think the judge would do?"

"Hard to say. I imagine he'll be relieved to be rid of the circus without a trial. That might have an impact."

Bob didn't say anything.

"How's the bar prep going?"

"Pretty well. I'll be ready."

"Good, good. We're all rooting for you."

"Thanks, Duane. Um, I need to get back to it," he said as he hung up.

He was, in fact, ready, though his confidence that he would pass the bar was interspersed with doubts about whether he even wanted to be a lawyer anymore. The exam itself, in mid-August, was tough, but he was fairly confident he had passed.

Soon after Marcus got home that day, Carol called.

"It's time to being Oscar Wilde home," Marcus told him when he hung up.

They drove up to LA that weekend. It was early September, with just a hint of fall in the air, and the breeze was a bit cooler, especially at night. They spent a lovely evening with Alex and Carol, who took them to their favorite Mexican restaurant in West Hollywood. After dinner they strolled down Santa Monica Boulevard, which was crowded with gay, straight, and undecipherable people.

At the breakfast table the next morning, Jay climbed into Marcus's lap.

"Can I come visit Oscar?" he asked.

Marcus smiled. "Of course you can. Any time you want."

Several of the puppies had already gone home, and Sophie was clearly not happy; she was anxiously watching over the remaining pups, Oscar and one other male. She gave Bob the saddest look when he lifted Oscar out of the pantry.

"Don't worry, momma," Bob said. "We'll take good care of him."

Sophie followed him out to the driveway, where Bob carefully placed Oscar in a small crate in the back seat while Marcus put their suitcases in the trunk. After a round of hugs they set out for home. The puppy whimpered a bit but soon fell asleep.

As soon they got home, they took Oscar to the patch of bark in the yard they had set aside for him; he sniffed around but didn't do anything. Marcus picked him up. Oscar promptly peed all over his pants.

82

The following Monday, Bob called Duane and set up a meeting for lunch.

He walked into the study, where Marcus was working at his desk with Oscar asleep at his feet. As he suspected would happen, Marcus became a doting doggy dad as soon as they brought the puppy home. Marcus even suggested they let Oscar sleep on their bed, but Bob put his foot down. They compromised on a doggy bed in their room, where, after the first week or so, Oscar slept contentedly. He did, however, wake up at the earliest sign of light in the morning, around 5:00 or so. He'd crawl out of his bed and sit next to theirs, breathing heavily. They took turns getting up to get him outside and then feed him. After his breakfast, he slept most of the morning. Marcus was always able to get back to sleep, Bob, never.

One sunny morning when Bob got up with Oscar the morning papers carried the story that Alexander Nelson had pled guilty to second-degree murder and was sentenced to fifteen years in prison.

"So that's that," Marcus said later in the morning, over coffee on the patio.

"How does it feel," he asked Bob, "to put a bad guy away?"

Bob shook his head. "I'm not sure. Strange."

That night they went back to the restaurant in Ocean Beach that they were beginning to think of as their place. It was a bit chillier now as the sun was setting, but after eating they walked out on the pier and watched the surfers, fewer in number now that the weather was cooler. Bob closed his eyes and inhaled deeply. He couldn't believe he had only been in San Diego for a few short months. It felt like years. The East coast seemed a million miles away.

"Let's go home," Marcus said. "I don't like leaving Oscar alone for too long."

Bob couldn't stop smiling. "I love you, Marcus," he said.

"Only for my body."

"Well, yeah, what did you think?"

Jason Thompson invited them to a party, where half the guests looked like him; the others were mostly doubles of Don Cade, the San Francisco escort and pornstar.

"Where do you find them?" Bob asked Jason, shaking his head.

"Oh, you know. Around."

They mingled, and did their best to blend in, but both felt very East coast-ish. They left early.

Oscar grew larger and would burst with joy whenever either of them came home, even if they had only been gone for a half hour. They hired a local dog-sitter to visit and play with him during the day when they were both gone, although Marcus worked at home as much as he could.

"It's not good to leave a child with a stranger too often," he said.

83

On the morning of his lunch with Duane, Bob played fetch with Oscar for a while, then barked out, "Enough already. Lie down."

Oscar looked contrite and lay at his feet. They had been working on obedience commands; Oscar was a quick learner.

He scratched the puppy's ear, remembering something his father had told him when he was considering challenging one of his professors about a law review article that Bob didn't think was good enough to publish, though the professor did.

"Bobby, you only play poker if you have some chips."

He smiled at the memory—he didn't challenge the professor—and put on his best suit. He now had some chips—valuable ones.

He met Duane at Fio's, a new Northern Italian restaurant in the Gaslamp District, San Diego's tourist mecca. He noticed a throng of business types at the restaurant's long bar.

"I'm not coming back," Bob said after they ordered.

Duane looked upset, but nodded.

"I want a year's severance, from today."

"That's a lot." Duane took off his glasses and rubbed the bridge of his nose.

Bob ignored him.

"I also want to see the letter of recommendation Fred promised to write, and promised to show me in advance, within two weeks."

Duane started to speak but Bob cut him off.

"In exchange for the severance and the letter, if it's good enough, I won't tell the press why I resigned, and how the investigation unfolded, including what I know about Fred and Amy." Bob paused. "And you."

Duane turned pale and took a sip of water. "Okay." He put his glasses back on, got up, and left.

Bob watched him leave. He felt calm, calmer than he had in weeks.

The waiter brought his risotto. He told the waiter to put Duane's meal in a doggy bag.

As he finished eating, Bob looked up and saw James Cunningham standing in front of him, smirking. He was carrying what looked like a double scotch.

"Mind if I join you?" he asked, not waiting for an answer before sitting in the other chair.

Bob said nothing and waited. Cunningham took a sip of his drink.

"So you've turned over a few rocks here in sunny California, and, goodness gracious, the things that have crawled out. Your poor, innocent Ivy League soul must feel tarnished."

Bob smiled and stared at him and kept his voice very calm. "Not at all. I chose criminal law. I knew I'd run into unsavory characters."

"Oh, *very* good," Cunningham chuckled. "You're learning fast. Keep working on that stare. It will come in handy in your line of work."

Bob said nothing more.

"Take care of yourself. And good luck," Cunningham said as he stood and plopped his empty glass on the table. His tone had changed; he sounded almost like a normal human being. "And if you ever decide to run for office, let us know. You could go far. Our newspapers could help."

He smiled—a real smile this time—and disappeared into the crowd at the bar.

Bob paid the check and left.

It was yet another gorgeous day, and he took a deep breath when he hit the sidewalk. He watched the crowd, mostly tourists, he guessed, before walking to the garage where he had parked his car.

At home he changed his clothes and took Oscar for a long walk. Oscar greeted everyone they met with his usual overwhelming excitement and deliriously wagging tale. The entire neighborhood seemed to love him.

When Marcus came home, he found Oscar napping in his bed and Bob in the bathtub with a glass of scotch.

"Oh, my. The scotch-in-the-bathtub routine. What's up?" he asked.

Bob told him everything. He hadn't been sure until the last minute he'd have the guts to go through with his demands, so he hadn't told Marcus anything about what he planned to do.

Marcus sat on the edge of the tub and rested his hand on top of Bob's, getting his shirt sleeve wet. He smiled.

"Okay."

84

In November, while Bob looked for another job, the Berlin Wall came down.

The next day, Amy Berkman held a press conference in front of a large crowd on the steps of City Hall. Her two children were at her side. Her makeup was heavier than usual.

Behind her was her new chief of staff, Cathy Anderson, formerly of the office of the San Diego District Attorney.

The mayor was wearing a stunning purple suit.

"The world is changing," she declared, "and we need bold, fresh leadership to take us into the future. The nineties will be challenging in so many ways, here in California and across this great nation. I want to meet those challenges, and that's why today I am announcing that I will seek the Republican nomination for the United States Senate."

The crowd cheered and Amy waved, one of her children on either side, waving with her.

Her smile was firmly in place.

Turn the Page for ...

a preview of *Rain*, H. N. Hirsch's next exciting mystery featuring Marcus and Bob, coming in 2024 from Pisgah Press.

RAIN

H.N. Hirsch

1

"Professor George, I'm about to be arrested for murder."

Professor Marcus George had just finished his lecture, loosened his tie, and was about to walk back to his office. He stepped outside into yet another perfect late afternoon in Southern California, temperature in the low 70s, warm sun, crisp breeze off the ocean. He inhaled deeply. The campus sat on a bluff overlooking the Pacific, and the smell and feel of the ocean was always in the air.

Marcus was looking forward to the drive home and changing into comfortable, loose-fitting shorts. He hated wearing a tie, but felt he needed it in large lecture courses like this one. He was teaching Ethics, a required course for first-year students in Earl Warren College, one of the several undergraduate colleges that made up the gigantic University of California, San Diego. Most of the students resented having to take the course, and Marcus learned quickly that he needed all the professorial authority he could muster.

He wanted to get home and play with Oscar, the five-year-old golden retriever that shared a home along with his partner Bob. Maybe they'd go out to dinner when Bob got home; they were both working hard these days and not much in the mood for cooking.

Kenny Glick, one of his graduate students, was waiting for him on the bench outside the lecture hall.

Rain

H.N. Hirsch

Marcus stared at him.

"Professor George?"

"Kenny, is this a joke?"

"I wish. I've just been questioned by the police. I think they're going to arrest me for murder."

<u>Mystery Fans:</u>

If you would like to be notified when Fault Line *will be available for purchase, please send your email address to PisgahPress@gmail.com with "Fault Line" as the subject.*

Acknowledgments

Heartfelt thanks to the indispensable editor Priscilla Long, to Ana Cara, Sandra Zagarell, Carter McAdams, John Burke, and Marilyn Malkin for reading drafts, and once again to A.D. Reed of Pisgah Press.

About the Author

H. N. Hirsch was born in Chicago and educated at the University of Michigan and at Princeton. A political scientist by training, he has been on the faculties of Harvard, the University of California-San Diego, Macalester College, and Oberlin, where he served as Dean of the Faculty and is now the Erwin N. Griswold Professor of Politics Emeritus. He is the author of *The Enigma of Felix Frankfurter* ("brilliant and sure to be controversial"—*The New York Times*), *A Theory of Liberty*, and the memoir *Office Hours* ("well crafted and wistful"—Kirkus), and numerous articles on law, politics, and constitutional questions.

About Pisgah Press

Pisgah Press was established in 2011 in Asheville, NC to publish works of quality offering original ideas and insight into the human condition and the world around us. If you support the old-fashioned tradition of publishing for the pleasure of the reader and the benefit of the author, please encourage your friends and colleagues to visit www.PisgahPress.com. For more information about *Shade* and other Pisgah Press books, contact us at pisgahpress@gmail.com.

CPSIA information can be obtained
at www.ICGtesting.com
Printed in the USA
BVHW091522110523
663997BV00020B/311